ELIZABETHAN MYSTERIES

Thief!

JOHN PILKINGTON

USBORNE

D0242543

ABERDEENSHIRE LIBRARY AND INFORMATION SERVICES	
2676126	
HJ	2655130
JF	£5.99
JU	JF

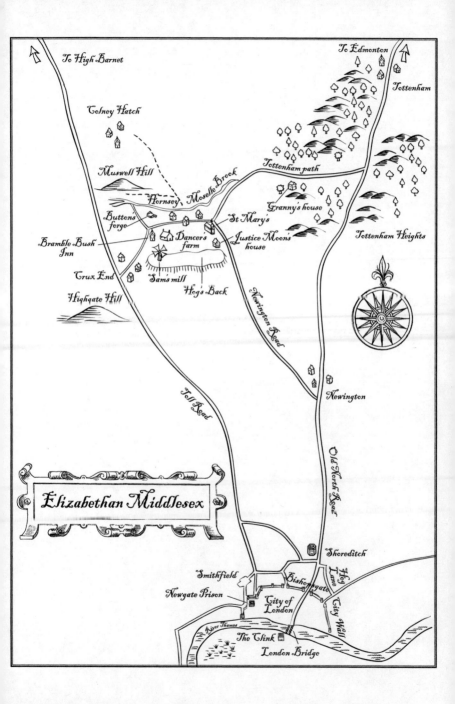

Thief!

ALIS

2676126

First published in the UK in 2009 by Usborne Publishing Ltd., Usborne House, 83-85 Saffron Hill, London EC1N 8RT, England. www.usborne.com

Copyright © John Pilkington, 2009

The right of John Pilkington to be identified as the author of this work has been asserted by him in accordance with the Copyright, Designs and Patents Act, 1988.

Cover artwork by James Goodbridge. Map by Ian McNee.

The name Usborne and the devices 🔱 🌐 are Trade Marks of Usborne Publishing Ltd.

All rights reserved. No part of this publication may be reproduced, stored in a retrieval system or transmitted in any form or by any means, electronic, mechanical, photocopying, recording or otherwise without the prior permission of the publisher.

This is a work of fiction. The characters, incidents, and dialogues are products of the author's imagination and are not to be construed as real. Any resemblance to actual events or persons, living or dead, is entirely coincidental.

A CIP catalogue record for this book is available from the British Library.

JFMAMJJAS ND/09 93063 ISBN 9780746097991 Printed in Great Britain.

Chapter One

Ben Button was coming home at last.

The air was bone-dry, and the countryside shimmered in summer heat. Ben was thirsty after his bumpy, three-mile cart-ride from Bishopsgate, but he didn't care. His excitement rose as Master Bowles hauled on the reins and drew his team of four plodding horses to a halt. They stood snorting in the dusty road, while insects flew about their heads. Bowles was the carrier who drove his heavily laden cart up the Old North Road once a fortnight, carrying goods from London to Lincoln, and sometimes all the way to York.

"Well, here's where you get down, young Ben." Master Bowles lifted his straw hat and wiped his brow. Raising his long whip, he pointed to a well-trodden path on the left. "There's a two-mile walk ahead of you – but you know that well enough, don't ye?"

Ben nodded, and climbed down eagerly from the cart. Just up the road was the hamlet of Newington, a cluster of small cottages. But Ben's way led north-west, down into Hornsey Vale, and his home village. It was more than twenty months since he had last been there.

For a moment he stood in the sunshine, taking in the view. To his right rose the tree-dotted slopes of Tottenham Heights, from where Tottenham Wood stretched northwards as far as Edmonton. Due west he could see Highgate Hill, a faint shape in the far distance. Before him lay fields of stubble. The hay crop had long been gathered, but new shoots had already sprouted up, and the second harvest, the *aftermath*, would take place before summer was over.

Ben hoped he would be able to stay long enough to help with the harvesting. He would have a lot of catching up to do – not just with his family, but with friends and neighbours too. His younger brother

Edward had been but a lad of nine when Ben had left home to be a player in the theatres. He would have turned eleven now, while their sister Margery was nine...

"Haven't you forgotten something?"

Startled out of his daydream, Ben looked round just in time to catch his pack as it was thrown down. "Thanks for the ride, Master Bowles," he said. "I wish you a safe journey."

Bowles waved, and his whip cracked as it snaked over the backs of the horses. With a loud creak and a jingle of harness the heavy cart lurched forward. Ben watched it draw away, until it was almost hidden in a cloud of dust.

He shouldered his pack and began to walk. Soon, thoughts of London and of his busy life as a boy player with Lord Bonner's company began to fade away. His master, John Symes, had sent a message ahead, telling Ben's mother that her son was coming to visit. Ben wondered if it had reached her. The messenger, a friend of John's, was riding to High Barnet, but had promised to turn aside and deliver the letter to Mistress Mary Button in Hornsey. Ben knew the man was trustworthy, yet he could not help feeling anxious. He wasn't really sure why – perhaps it was because he had been away for so long.

He knew he had grown up quite a lot since his family had last seen him. He had been through a few adventures in that time, and he had changed: from a country lad, to a seasoned performer on the stage. He had even played before the Queen herself... But that thought made Ben uneasy. To speak of such things might seem like boasting to the plain folk of Hornsey. He decided not to say too much about his life in London, unless people asked him.

The path had dipped, and to Ben's left a large, brick-and-timber house came into view, set back on the hillside. It was always a surprise to stumble upon Justice Moon's house, which was rather isolated, with only fields about it. Ben had known Richard Moon most of his life although, like many village folk, he had rarely seen the man. He was the local magistrate who was supposed to keep the peace in the district, but he kept mostly to himself, with little time for worldly affairs. What mattered more to Justice Moon than anything else were his scientific investigations. He had a laboratory in his house, which was said to have strange things in it. Some people were fearful of the man, suspecting him of dabbling in dangerous matters – even witchcraft. Others thought Moon was merely a dotty old fool, who neglected his duties in favour of his books and experiments.

There was no doubt that he neglected his house, Ben thought. The timber frame was in need of repair, while the brickwork was crumbling in places. The garden was overgrown, with the trunk of a fallen tree almost blocking the gateway. Beside the weed-choked path which led round to the stables was a small paddock, where a rather sad-looking horse stood, staring at Ben over a fence.

Ben stopped to gaze at the justice's old house. The place looked so rundown, it was as if nobody lived there. But there was a horse, so someone must be home... Then movement caught his eye.

Someone *was* home. In fact this someone – who was not Justice Moon, but a blond-haired lad in a grubby shirt and breeches – had appeared from behind the house and was staring at Ben in a rather unfriendly manner.

"What're you looking at?" he demanded. When Ben gave no answer the boy came forward, hopped over the fallen tree and halted a few yards away. He was barefoot. "I said what—" he began, but Ben cut him short.

"I heard what you said. I was looking at the horse, if you must know. He looks thirsty."

The blond boy glared. "I gave him a drink not an hour ago," he answered. "He wants for nothing...and who are you to stick your nose in? The justice don't like visitors!"

Ben sighed. He had played many roles in the past year and a half – even soldiers, when the company was short of hired men. He knew all about looking fierce – "strutting peacock-fashion", the players called it.

"My name's Button," he said. "And I'm Hornsey born and bred. I'd say I've as much right to ask about the justice's horse as anyone, wouldn't you?"

At that the boy's expression changed. "Button?" He gave a start. "Not the blacksmith's boy...the one who ran off to join the travelling players?"

Ben frowned. "My father was the blacksmith in Hornsey, once," he replied. "But I didn't run off..."

"You're Edward Button's brother!" the blond boy cried. "'Twas you sent the brindled cow!"

"Well, that's true," Ben admitted. The cow that had been sent to his mother was a reward, given to Ben by a rich knight whose life he had saved, back in the springtime. But he had no wish to speak of that – especially since the knight in question had ended up losing his head, which as far as Ben knew was still stuck on a pole above the south gatehouse of London Bridge.

But when the other boy spoke again, Ben began to feel rather uncomfortable.

"Some say you're dead, did you know that? A peddler who came by last winter claimed you was locked up in the Clink prison – that's in London, isn't it? And then you got stabbed, and bled to death by a pike pond—"

"Wait!" Ben protested. "I was never in prison, nor was I stabbed. Well…I mean, I got a cut, but—"

"Where?" the blond lad asked. "Is there a scar?"

"Hold your peace, will you?" Ben said, somewhat exasperated. "And who are you, anyway? I don't remember your face."

"I'm Hal," came the reply. "Hal Faraway. Nor would you remember me. I'm not from Hornsey – nor from anywhere I know of. I'm from far away, that's all. That's why the justice named me so."

Ben gazed at Hal Faraway. Now that he had dropped his air of bravado, he seemed civil enough. His face and hands were dirty from hard work, perhaps in the stables.

"He named you?" Ben repeated. "You mean you work here, for Justice Moon?"

"I do," Hal answered. "Since he saw me at Barnet Horse Fair last year, and brought me home. 'Being a skipjack's no life for a promising lad,' he said. And he

needed someone about the place, after his man left."
He shrugged. "My bed's but a heap of straw in the
stable loft, but it's better than what I had."

Skipjacks were the boys who worked for the horse
dealers that travelled about the country. Ben knew
that life for these boys was hard, for many of the men
who bought and sold horses were rough fellows, who
did not scruple to break the law. Hal might have been
harshly treated.

"So you've come home, Button... Well, that'll
surprise some folk. Sure as I'm standing here, it
will!" Hal looked rather crafty now, as if he knew
things Ben didn't.

"My mother knows I'm coming," Ben said. "My
master sent a message."

"That's good." Hal nodded. "I mean, it's good she
knows..." Quickly he looked away.

"Is there something I should know too?" Ben asked.
"Because if there is, I'd be glad if you told me."

Hal merely shrugged. "It's none of my affair," he
said. "You'll find out soon enough."

But feeling uneasy now, Ben took a step forward,
which made the other boy tense at once. "Here – you
wouldn't want to tangle with me," he said in a
warning tone. "I've won prizes at wrestling matches,
I have!"

"Then I'll have to be careful," Ben replied. "Or I might forget myself, and fall back to my sword-and-dagger training." He patted his belt, where his poniard – his small dagger – was sheathed. It was fit for little more than cutting bread and fruit, but it looked menacing enough.

Hal's eyes narrowed. "I wouldn't advise that, either," he muttered. "When I was at the fairs, I dealt with folk who'd have chewed you up and spat out the pieces!"

Then, catching the look on Ben's face, Hal let out a breath. "There's no call to mock me, master player," he said in a rueful tone. "I don't want to fight you." He hesitated. "I didn't want to be the one who told you, that's all."

"But you haven't told me anything," Ben said impatiently. "Has something happened to one of my family?"

To his relief, Hal Faraway shook his head. "Nothing's happened," he said. "Or, nothing for you to fret about. It's...well, it's Dancer May you should be asking, not me." But with that, Hal realized he had said too much. For at mention of the name, Ben's face fell.

"Dancer? What about him?"

Again Hal hesitated. "Very well, since you've

pressed me," he replied at last. "Everyone knows it anyway – but you didn't hear this from me." Hal drew a long breath, then said: "Dancer May has been paying court to your mother since early springtime. From what I hear, he means to make her his wife."

The boy turned and hopped over the fallen tree. Then without looking back, he walked off round the corner of the house.

For a while Ben stood on the pathway outside Justice Moon's. The horse had wandered away and was cropping grass, but he didn't notice. A crow flew overhead, cawing raucously, but he didn't hear it. Nor did he hear the wasp that appeared from somewhere, buzzing in a menacing fashion. All he heard were Hal Faraway's words:

Dancer May has been paying court to your mother... *He means to make her his wife...*

Ben's mouth was dry, and it wasn't just the heat that caused it. Henry May, a widowed farmer, who owned some of the best pastureland in the Vale, was known to everyone as Dancer – and he was the only man in the village Ben truly disliked.

The feeling went back years, to the time Dancer had accused Ben of throwing stones at his geese – something Ben would never have done. And even though the real culprit was soon found, Dancer had never said he was sorry. He thought himself too important, Ben had decided – perhaps that was why his father had never liked Dancer, either. And now this man was courting Ben's mother... Could it really be true?

Something tickled his arm, and he looked down to see a wasp had settled on it. He flicked it away, before turning at last from the house...but, as he did so, there came a sudden flash of light, so bright that it made Ben blink. It was gone in an instant.

Ben looked round, trying to see where the flash had come from. But there was only the old tumbledown house before him, with butterflies flitting about the overgrown flower beds. Then, thinking he saw a tiny movement from the first floor, he glanced up. The morning sunlight reflected off the windows – perhaps it was nothing more. Yet Ben could not help feeling that he had been watched. Had someone been there? Could it even have been Justice Moon himself?

He frowned, as his thoughts turned back to what Hal Faraway had said. He shifted his pack and began trudging down the path to Hornsey again.

No one saw him as he walked. But if anyone had, they would have noticed how the spring had gone from his step. And that was how he arrived in

Hornsey village a short while later, to see the familiar street with its timber-and-thatch cottages.

But it was not the homecoming he had expected... not by a very long chalk indeed.

Chapter Two

As soon as Mary Button saw Ben walking up to the cottage, she gave a cry and dropped the pail she was carrying. Luckily it was empty, or its contents would have spilled across the doorstep. She hurried forward, grabbed her son and squeezed him tightly. Then she leaned back, holding him by the shoulders, and stared at him.

"By the heavens, how you've grown!" she exclaimed. "Your brother and sister will hardly recognize you!"

Then she sniffed and wiped her nose – and Ben

was surprised to find his own tears welling up. He looked into his mother's face, at her soft grey eyes which looked keenly into his.

"Are you in health?" she asked. "You must be tired – did you walk all the way from London?"

"I had a ride to Newington, Mother. I'm fine." Ben smiled. The worrying thoughts that had beset him since his meeting with Hal Faraway were fading. Instead, a warm glow was stealing over him. He was really home.

There came a shout, and a figure in a loose smock hurtled out of the house towards him. Ben had barely time to look before Margery threw herself against him.

"I said you'd come before midday!" she cried. "Edward said you were a city boy now, and it'd take you all day to get here – but I knew different!"

Ben hugged his sister, then drew back to gaze at her. He wasn't the only one who had grown, he thought – though Margery's face had not changed. Her cheeks were red, her brown hair sun-bleached where it poked from under her linen hood. Like their mother, she was grinning from ear to ear.

"Tell us about London!" she urged. "Have you really met the Queen?"

"I didn't meet her," Ben answered, feeling

embarrassed now. "I mean, I've bowed to her and everything—"

"Well, that's as good as meeting her, isn't it?"

Mary put an arm round her daughter's shoulders. "There'll be plenty of time for tales...let's go inside and take some dinner." She threw a knowing look at Margery. "We've a surprise for Ben, haven't we?"

"It's our own cheese, made from Eliza's milk!" Margery cried – then gasped.

Ben couldn't help laughing. "You've let the cat out of the bag, haven't you," he said. "Would Eliza be the cow's name, by any chance?"

"Margery named her," Mother said with a smile. "You'll see her soon enough..." She glanced over Ben's shoulder and he looked round to see people gathering in the street. One or two waved at him and someone called out, "It's good to see you back, young Ben!"

Ben waved, but Margery was tugging at his sleeve. "Come in," she urged. "Or you'll be out here all day!"

"She's right," Mary said, and with a wave to the neighbours, she turned to the cottage. "You can catch up with the gossip later – first you must eat and drink." So, with Margery on his arm, Ben followed his mother to the doorway. All at once there was so much to say, he did not know where to begin.

"Where's Edward?" he asked. "Isn't he here?"

Mother had stepped inside. But Margery leaned close to Ben. "He's helping out at Dancer May's," she said. "He's there most days…" Then seeing his startled look, she lowered her voice.

"Don't ask Mother about that," she muttered. "There's something you must know first, about Dancer."

Ben spoke softly too. "I've already heard—" he began, but Margery put a finger to her lips. Then she pushed past Ben, and hurried indoors.

A half-hour later, dinner was over. It had been plain country fare, but to Ben it was as good as a feast.

"That's the best cheese I've eaten in months," he told his mother. "And I don't say that just because you've made it."

Mary smiled as she rose from the table. Margery jumped up to help, but her mother stopped her. "Perhaps you'd like to show Eliza to Ben now," she added. "After all, it's thanks to him we have a cow, isn't it?"

Margery nodded eagerly, while Ben smiled and got up to follow her out. As he went he glanced at their mother, but she was busy, with her back to him, collecting up the platters.

His smile faded. Though the meal had been lively enough, with Margery pressing him about his life in London, Ben noticed that his mother had not said much. But then he had been taken aback himself, though he did his best not to show it. What had shocked him was how shabby the cottage looked.

It was clean, of course – his mother had always kept a good house – but it was obvious the place was in need of improving. For the first time, Ben realized, he was seeing clear signs of his family's poverty, and it troubled him.

After Margery's warning, he had kept off the subject of Dancer May. But the unease he had felt on hearing the news from Hal Faraway had not disappeared. Stepping outside into the sunshine, he resolved to find out all he could from Margery – and the sooner the better.

The Buttons' cottage was small but sturdy, roofed with thatch like the other houses in the village. Its oak frame was infilled with walls of wattle plastered with clay. Downstairs was a single room which served as kitchen, parlour and everything else, with a stair leading to the upper floor. And to one side of the house was the old forge, where Ben's father had once practised his craft as the village blacksmith.

Peter Button had died of some unknown sickness nearly five years ago now. Margery, who had been a small child, barely remembered their father. But Ben, who had been nine at that time of sadness, had many memories. And even though the forge was just an outhouse now, and the furnace had long been cold and silent, Ben could still picture his father, his blond hair tied back, standing by the entrance. Master Button, a quiet and modest man, was still missed. Perhaps that was why no one had wanted to take over the blacksmith's. Nowadays, those who needed tools mended or horses shod had to walk over a mile to the neighbouring village of Crux End.

Ben stepped under the low beam into shadow, and grew aware of a familiar country smell – of cow. For now, of course, the forge served as a dairy. A milkmaid's stool and a wooden churn stood against one wall, and from the hooks where blacksmith's tools had once hung, jugs and ladles dangled. Through the back door, which was half open, Ben could see the chicken pen, and hear the squawks of the hens...

"Here she is! Isn't she splendid?"

His sister's voice rang out in the gloom. As Ben's eyes adjusted to it, he heard the dull thud of hooves

on straw. Beside Margery he saw a dark shape –
bigger than he'd expected.

"She's enormous!" he exclaimed. For though he
had requested a cow as his reward, in fact, he had
never seen it.

"She gives ten pints of milk nearly every time –
sometimes more!" Margery stood proudly beside
Eliza, patting the cow's thick, acorn-brown coat.
"Mother lets me do the milking by myself – you can
watch me later." She gestured towards the back door.
"We put her out to graze on the common, but Mother
said I could bring her in today, just to show you."

Eliza turned her head and gazed at Ben with huge
brown eyes. And he couldn't help but feel a surge of
pride that he had been responsible for her arrival. He
knew that the cow's milk, let alone the butter and
cheese it could produce, must have made a difference
to his family. As if reading his thoughts, Margery
smiled.

"We sell the butter in London," she said. "Ellen
May takes it to East Cheap Market once a week, with
the eggs and the vegetables..."

Then she broke off. Ellen May, a young woman
of eighteen, was the daughter of Dancer May: the
man whose name had not been spoken again since
Ben arrived.

"I was going to ask you about Dancer," Ben said. "Now's as good a time as any, isn't it?" And quickly he told Margery what he had learned from Hal Faraway. At once, her face clouded.

"I don't think there's anything to be done," she said. "If Mother goes and marries Dancer, he'll be stepfather to all of us – whether we want it or not.

"I wish her only happiness," Margery went on. "And Dancer seems to make her happy. At least, she smiles more than she used to. And Edward likes him—"

"But you don't – any more than I do," Ben broke in.

His sister sighed. "I've tried to see the best in him..." She hesitated. "But I can't help it, Ben. I think what Dancer really wants is our house, and our bit of land."

Ben frowned. "Dancer's got more acres than most farmers round here!"

"You don't understand," Margery said with a shake of her head. "If he and Mother marry, he wants us all to go and live with him and Ellen at the farm. Then we could lease out the cottage and the forge, he says – to a new blacksmith. We'd have the rent money, and Hornsey would have a smith again. Everyone wins, Dancer says." She began stroking the cow's coat. "At least Eliza can come with us," she added sadly. "He knows we wouldn't give her up for anything!"

"But we don't need to move!" Ben cried. He could hardly believe his ears – suddenly it looked as if his house, along with everything he knew, was in danger of being taken away. The thought of someone else living in his family's home shocked him. He had never imagined it possible.

Margery was gazing at him. "It makes me sad too," she said. "And there's been no one I could talk to about it – until you came home."

She took Ben's hand and squeezed it. And all he could do was squeeze back.

Ben's brother Edward returned just before supper time. He had been doing odd jobs at Dancer's farm south of the village, and he was tired, his face streaked with dirt. To Ben's surprise Edward barely greeted him, but went round the back of the cottage to wash. At a glance from his mother, Ben followed.

He walked by the chicken pen, where the hens strutted about pecking at the ground. Edward had pulled off his shirt and was splashing water over himself from a pail. When Ben realized that Edward was not going to speak, he made an effort himself.

"I hardly knew you when you came in just now," he said. "You've grown so much."

It was true. Edward was almost as tall as Ben, and looked older than his eleven years. In fact he had a different look about him from when Ben had last seen him – rather stern, Ben thought. It was as if – having been without a father for so long, and without an older brother – Edward saw himself as not only grown up, but somehow in charge, too.

"Ah, well – it's the country air that does that," he replied, straightening up. "Country air and hard work – not what you're used to in London, I dare say."

He gazed at Ben before bending to wash his face.

"It's harder work in the theatres than you might think," Ben said. "Matt Fields and I – he's the other boy player – we've many jobs to do. Apart from the acting I mean..."

At this Edward looked up – and didn't try to hide the scorn on his face. "Acting!" he snorted. "You don't call that work, do you? And look how you're dressed!"

He gestured at Ben's linen shirt, with its falling band of lace. It was as well he was not wearing his crimson doublet, in the livery of his patron, Lord Bonner. All of a sudden even his grey hose looked fancy, compared with Edward's patched work breeches.

"My master bought me a new shirt to come home in," Ben retorted. He had never known Edward to be spiteful before. "I don't have a wage—"

But Edward snatched up his own shirt, which was plain and work-stained, and began rubbing himself dry with it.

"Pity you didn't get home in time for the hay harvest. That was real work – everyone had to pitch in. Dancer let me drive the cart once." Then seeing the look that came over Ben's face, his brother lowered his gaze.

"He's been good to us, Dancer has," he went on. "You don't know how hard it's been for Mother, trying to keep things going on her own. She sold the pig last autumn, didn't you notice?"

Ben managed a nod. "I was going to ask about it," he said. "I haven't had the chance yet." Then another thought struck him. "Father's old tools – have they been sold too?" he asked in dismay.

Edward nodded. He had finished drying himself, and ran a hand through his untidy hair. "Mother had no choice," he replied. "She works harder than ever, with the garden, the hens and churning butter and everything. Margery does what she can – she's learning how to spin flax, from Widow Luce. And when Dancer said he wanted me to help at the farm, I stopped going to those lessons the parson was giving at the church. Not that I minded – I wasn't learning anything. We need every penny we can get!"

Ben was feeling worse by the minute. "I thought the cow would help," he murmured. But whatever he said, it did not seem to matter. Edward made him feel as if he had simply abandoned his family for the life of a player.

Edward hesitated. "It was a good thought," he allowed. "Mother was pleased. Even though we couldn't work out what you'd done to get it. The drovers who brought it here didn't say much."

Suddenly Ben was tempted to tell Edward the whole story: how he had saved a man from a dagger thrust, at the risk of getting stabbed himself. But instead he said, "Was it you who spread the word I'd run off with travelling players?"

Edward shrugged. "Well, didn't you?"

Ben opened his mouth. He wanted to remind Edward that their mother had agreed to his joining Lord Bonner's Men – but the words stuck in his throat.

"How long is it you're staying, anyway?" Edward asked, putting his shirt back on.

"I don't know. The company's just come back from touring," Ben answered, still smarting from his brother's words. "They're taking a rest until we start playing at the Curtain. That's a theatre in Shoreditch," he added, though he doubted Edward was interested. "My master will come and fetch me when he's ready."

"So you might miss the second harvest, too," Edward said with a thin smile. "That's good timing, isn't it?"

"It was the only time off I could get!" Ben cried. He was angry now. Like a lot of brothers, the Button boys sometimes quarrelled, but Edward's sneering had got the better of Ben. They had been in each other's company for less than an hour; what would things be like in a day or two? he wondered.

Edward picked up the pail and carried it past Ben, towards their mother's vegetable patch. As he did so, a little of the dirty water slopped over the side onto Ben's shoes. Ben stepped back and Edward brushed past him.

"Mustn't waste this – it goes on the garden," Edward said, then he glanced down. "Sorry, did I splash your city shoes? Clumsy of me – we country lads can be a bit coarse, can't we?"

He busied himself, setting the pail down beside the

rows of beans and covering it with a wooden lid.

Ben turned and walked back round the house. For the first time since he had arrived in the village, he felt utterly unwelcome.

But worse was yet to come; for at sunset, Dancer May came to visit.

Chapter Three

*D*ancer was an odd sort of man for a farmer. Ever since Ben could remember him he had shone at village fairs, showing off his dancing steps, which was how he got his nickname. Yet most of the time he moved slowly and talked slowly, and he would not be interrupted until he had finished what he had to say. When he arrived at the Buttons' cottage that evening he had a lot to say – none of it to Ben's liking.

"So, what parts do ye play on the stage, young Ben?" Dancer asked, setting down his mug of Mary

Button's home-brewed ale. "Is it true what I've heard – that boys must play the women, flouncing about in dresses?"

Ben blinked. He and Edward were sitting on one side of the table, with Mother and Margery at the other. Dancer had taken a stool at the end of the table, where he sat as if he were already head of the family. It made Ben feel tense.

"I take women's roles, as well as others," he answered quietly. "And I play the lute, and sing and dance..."

He broke off as a grin formed on Dancer's broad face. He put a hand to his chin, and rubbed his thick brown beard.

"You dance? Well, that's good. Though in the country, dancing's what we do on holidays. I never knew you could get paid for it!"

Ben said nothing. Beside him he heard Edward snigger. Opposite, Margery sat with her eyes lowered. It was left to their mother to speak.

"Ben's a prentice, Dancer," she said with a slight frown. "He gets bed and board at his master's, and his clothes, but no more."

Dancer turned to her. "So that's why he sends nothing home to his family," he murmured. And before Mary could reply, he faced Ben. "Your mother's too kind to say it, young man," he went on, "so let me say it for her." He was no longer smiling. As the others watched, he lifted his mug slowly and took another drink before lowering it again.

"A theatre's no place for a true Englishman," Dancer said. "Everyone knows players are rogues and liars – too lazy to do an honest day's toil. Folk hereabouts think you should come home, and do some proper work."

A silence had fallen. His heart thumping, Ben met Dancer's eye. And he did not look away when the man said:

"So – I've a proposition for ye. Maybe your mother's told you already, but I'll spell it out: I wish to take her for my wife. She's been a widow long enough – and paid the price with her poverty. And if she accepts my hand – as I dare hope she will – then I think you'll see that it opens a new door for her children, too."

He smiled at Mary Button, but she did not meet his eye. Turning to Ben, she said: "I was going to tell you this evening, but Dancer can put it better than I."

"Aye – so here's my offer," Dancer said, his eyes on Ben again. "If – nay, *when*, Mary and I marry, there's a home for you at the farm, along with your brother and sister. And a future, too," he added, with a glance at Edward. "For you know I've no sons to carry on after me. It's likely Ellen will marry one day, and make her own life." He paused, letting Ben take the words in.

"Farm work's hard, and the hours are long – but ye know that well enough," Dancer went on. "There's much ye'd have to learn, but the farmyard will be your school. It's better than anything the parson's got!" He spoke of Master Harrington, the parson of St Mary's Church, who taught local children at his own expense.

"So there's your choice, Ben Button..." Dancer was staring hard at him. "Will you do right by your mother and me – stay home in Hornsey, and be a part of our family?" A smile spread over his features. "But I'm forgetting: you'd no longer be Ben Button. You'd have my name – you'd be Ben May. It's a name I've been proud to bear, all my life. And a May would live on to farm my acres, after I'm dead and gone!"

Dancer sat back contentedly, but if anyone thought he had finished they were mistaken. For without taking his eyes off Ben, he added: "Or, do you mean to go back to London, and strut about on the stage like a fool all your life, for the amusement of city folk?" Then as if to mark the end of his speech he banged a hand on the table.

"So, young Ben," cried Dancer, "what do you say?"

The silence was like a weight pressing Ben down. Outside he could hear the hens clucking. In the cottage all was still as he made his answer. He knew it wasn't the one Dancer expected, but he gave it all the same.

"I'm neither a fool nor a liar," he said. "Nor is my master, nor any of my company. We're servants to the Lord Bonner, and have played before the Queen. We're admired by folk of all classes – and beyond London, when we take our plays to villages much farther off than this. People there are glad to see real entertainment – not just country folk hopping about on the green—"

"Ben!"

His mother's voice came sharply, and Ben knew he had let his tongue run away with him. Yet Dancer's words had filled him with shame. In London he was proud to be a member of one of the best companies of players. He was not laughed at, except when he played comic roles and such laughter was welcome. But here, all he had achieved seemed to count for nothing – at least to Dancer and Edward. With the colour rising to his cheeks, Ben looked across the table.

"Your pardon, Mother," he muttered. "I…" But he could not find the words. He wanted to say how hurt he was – not just for himself, but for his father too. The thought of giving up his name filled Ben with dismay. It would be as if the Buttons had never existed…and the worst part was, no one looked as unhappy as he was. Even Margery seemed to think that if their mother wished to marry Dancer, they must accept it – though it meant giving up almost everything they had, and living as Dancer's family for ever!

"It's not me you should ask pardon from!" his mother said. She sounded indignant, but Ben knew she was not angry with him. She was worried. He had already begun to see how hard life had been for her these past years. Now he felt more ashamed and unhappy, for he guessed that his mother really wanted what Dancer wanted: that Ben give up acting and stay with his family. Then she could watch him grow up along with Edward and Margery, and they would have a good home, with no more fears about money.

All eyes were on Ben. His earlier excitement about coming home had disappeared with the realization that he now had a new struggle to face. Although there had always been a likelihood his mother would remarry, Ben had never imagined it would happen this way. But there was little he could do – for it seemed as if everything had been decided in his absence.

"I beg your pardon," he said to Dancer. "I meant not to be rude, nor to seem ungrateful. I know you've been a good friend to my mother, and I'll do my best to make amends."

Then he lowered his eyes. He barely heard Dancer saying, "Well...that was said with good grace," and adding he would forget all about the matter. "In any case," Dancer sighed, "since it's growing dark, I'd better be getting back to the farm. I'll see you tomorrow, Edward, and perhaps you too, Ben?"

But Ben kept his eyes on the table. Dancer may wish to forget about the matter – but he could not.

In the night Ben was woken by the cry of a bird – a nightjar, perhaps? For a moment he thought he was in his attic room at the Symes's house in Hog Lane... Then someone nearby grunted, and Ben remembered where he was. On the other straw pallet, Edward turned in his sleep. Beyond the thin wall that divided the upper floor of the cottage in two, their mother and Margery slept, no doubt soundly. Only Ben lay awake, thinking over what had happened.

Alone in the dark, he found himself facing an impossible choice. On the one hand he could bow to his mother's wishes, give up his life as a player and stay to become a farmer's boy like Edward, living under Dancer's roof. On the other hand, if he refused and returned to London he would be like an outcast in his own family, with no real home to return to. Either way, he would be unhappy. He loved the acting life – Lord Bonner's Men were like a second family to him. But his real family was here, and they missed him – or at least, his mother and Margery did. Now, he realized how much he had missed them, too.

He turned over and tried to sleep, but he kept seeing Dancer's stern face as he told Ben the theatre was *no place for a true Englishman*. Ben still smarted from that. There were no truer Englishmen than Lord Bonners' Players, he thought, as memories sprang up: his master John Symes, the company's leader, who was wise and fair, and would stand up to anyone; prickly Gabriel Tucker, with his moustache and his hot temper; "Handsome Hugh" Cotton with his easy smile; Solomon Tree with his long face and his dry wit; grumpy Will Sanders who wished no one any real harm – and of course his best friend, Matt Fields, who had shared many adventures with him. Suddenly Ben missed them all. He could always tell them his troubles, no matter what they were. He wondered what John would have said. But he knew even John could not advise him this time. Ben sighed – whereupon a voice from the darkness startled him.

"Can't you sleep?"

Edward spoke softly. Ben could not see him, but he knew his brother was lying on his side facing him.

"I did, for a while," Ben answered. He half-expected another taunt, but was taken aback when Edward said: "I forgot to tell you: there's something else you should know. It's about Granny Jenkin."

"I was going to see Granny tomorrow," Ben said. "What is it? Is she unwell?"

"I don't know," Edward muttered. "But Mother's worried about her. She's been acting strange these past few days."

"How do you mean?" Ben asked. Granny Jenkin was their only surviving grandparent, their mother's mother, who lived alone in a cottage by the path to Tottenham.

"She didn't come into the village this week," Edward replied. "She always comes in summertime, to sit outside the inn and gossip, but she stayed home." He gave a yawn. "Mother walked over to see her two days ago, but Granny wouldn't open the door. She was talking nonsense, Mother said. If you ask me, the old bird's going soft in the head."

Ben gave a start. "Then why doesn't someone try and help her?"

Edward sniffed. "What can they do? Who could take her in, let alone look after her? We haven't the room, have we?" He hesitated, then added: "Dancer won't have her at the farm. He's told Mother he couldn't find room for her as well as us."

"Do you always do what Dancer says?" Ben retorted. The words were out before he could stop them – yet he did not want to stop them.

But all Edward said was, "You know what Dancer told you makes sense. He's offering us a new home – have you got any better ideas?"

Ben made no reply. He heard Edward let out a sigh and turn away. Soon his snores began to fill the room.

After a while Ben drifted off into a troubled sleep. When he woke again the first rays of sunrise were poking through the small window, and he decided to get up. He wanted to rise early, before Edward. But when he came downstairs, he found Mary Button already there.

The fire was lit and porridge simmered in a pot.

When Ben appeared, his mother merely nodded and told him to sit down. He did so, feeling empty – and not just from hunger. When she brought him a bowl of porridge and asked him what he planned to do that day, Ben said at once that he would visit Granny Jenkin.

"It's a good idea," Mother said, although a frown puckered her brow. "But don't be put out if she doesn't make you welcome. Granny's not been herself of late."

"Edward told me," Ben said. Then he looked away and picked up his spoon.

He did not know what to say to his mother – but from the look on her face, nor did she know what to say to him.

The village was stirring as Ben made his way along the dusty, rutted street. Doors were open, and people greeted him warmly. Since the population of Hornsey was barely a hundred people, and Ben knew every one of them, he could have had enough conversations to last him all morning. So, promising everybody he met that he would see them soon, he walked past the church and took the path that led north-east, to Tottenham Wood.

It was going to be another hot day. Cows and goats stood on the common, in the shade of its few trees. A horse, tethered on a long rope, was twitching its tail to keep flies away. Birds flew everywhere: crows, lapwings, ouzels and skylarks...they were as familiar to Ben as always. There was no denying he was still a country lad, who sprang from country folk on both sides of his family. Granny Jenkin, for one, had never been far from the village. She had always said she only went to London once, to see Queen Elizabeth ride to her coronation. That was long ago, Ben knew – back in 1559, when Granny had been a much younger woman. Now she was near her sixtieth year, somewhat stiff and a little deaf. Yet she had never lost the sparkle in her eye...and thinking of what he had heard from Edward, Ben hoped she had not lost it still. Feeling rather anxious, he followed the path uphill away from the village, and the trees began to close round him.

Ben barely remembered Granny's husband, his grandfather. He had been a ploughman, a shy fellow who preferred the company of horses to people. Grandfather and Granny Jenkin had always lived outside the village, in the cottage where they had brought up their family: Ben's mother and her sisters, who were both married and far off. But Granny still grew herbs and fruits on her little patch of land, and seemed content. Until now, perhaps, Ben thought... Then he saw the cottage ahead, and quickened his pace. But when he rounded its corner to the doorway, he stopped abruptly.

Something was wrong.

He did not know what it was. Granny's house in the clearing looked as it always did. The old crab-apple tree stood at the front, positioned to catch the sunlight, beside the gooseberries and the strawberry bed. The cottage was in good repair, the thatch firm, for there were always folk who would help Granny out in return for a basket of fruit or a jar of her preserves. Still Ben stood in the garden where bees buzzed about, trying to decide what it was that made him uneasy. Then a loud creak startled him – and the door opened abruptly.

"Get away from here!" a shrill voice cried. "Off with you!"

Ben's mouth fell open. "Granny?" He stepped towards the doorway. "It's Ben – I've come to visit."

The door was open a few inches, but the inside of the house was dark. Only then did Ben notice that the front windows were shuttered. His alarm growing, he took another pace – but was pulled up short. This time Granny's voice was almost a shriek.

"I said get away!" she yelled. "You're not wanted! Leave me alone – or it'll be the worse for you!"

Ben could just make out a face in the crack between the door and its frame, though he could not even be sure it was Granny's. But her words were clear enough.

"Granny – what's wrong?" he asked. "Don't you know me? It's Ben – I'm back from London—"

Immediately the door was banged shut. The wood fell silent, apart from a few birds flying away, startled by the noise. In dismay, Ben gazed at the door. He thought of hammering on it. As his mother had said, Granny was not herself. Perhaps she had lived alone too long, out here in the wood?

Still he stood there, half hoping the door would open again, and his grandmother would come out and tell him she was sorry. Of course she knew him, she would say, and he must come in and have some of her famous damson tart, and tell him his news...

But it did not happen. And somehow he knew it was not going to happen. Unable to bear it any longer, he stepped right up to the door and knocked loudly, but there was no answer. He knocked again, then tried the handle, but the door must have been barred from within, for it would not open. He listened, but the house was silent.

He sighed. Now he had someone else to worry about: not only Edward and Dancer, but Granny too. With a heavy heart, he turned and began to retrace his steps through the trees.

Chapter Four

*B*en took a roundabout route back to the cottage, to collect his thoughts. He passed through the fields north of Hornsey, crossing the old path to Colney Hatch and making a wide semicircle, almost as far as Muswell Hill. For a while he watched a man flying a hawk, the hill being a favourite spot for falconers. Then he walked homewards, crossed the brook by stepping stones and came round by the back of the forge. He went inside and found his mother churning butter.

She looked up without breaking her steady rhythm.

Edward was gone to Dancer's, she said, while Margery had milked Eliza and taken her to the common. Then she asked about Ben's visit to Granny's so, sadly, he told his tale.

His mother listened, as she worked the wooden pole in an up-and-down motion in the churn. "She sounds worse," she said, when Ben had finished. "I must think what to do."

On his walk Ben had been thinking about it too. "Someone should go to her cottage soon," he said. "Even if they have to force their way in. She might not be looking after herself properly."

His mother stopped working. "She's getting old and forgetful, that's all," she said. The two of them gazed at each other, until finally Mary looked away. She began churning again, more vigorously than before.

"I know I should have sent word to you sooner," she said. "I mean about Dancer...but I believe what I'm doing is for the best. I have to think of Edward and Margery. It's been a struggle to provide for them, since...well, these last years. I think you're old enough to understand that, Ben."

Ben could think of nothing to say.

"Once we're settled at the farm," his mother went on briskly, "I'll speak to Dancer again about Granny.

He might come round." She turned suddenly. "He's not a bad man," she said. "You shouldn't think harshly of him. I owe him a great deal – we all do."

"I know," Ben said. But he wanted to say more – about giving up his father's name, for a start. Not to mention losing the cottage, and having to obey Dancer for the rest of his days, or at least until he was old enough to set up a home of his own.

Mother stopped again, and now there was sadness in her gaze. "I know it troubles you," she murmured. "Yet sometimes our lives don't go as we wish them to. Will you try to make the best of it, for my sake?"

"Of course I will, Mother," Ben replied, though his heart felt like a stone sinking in a pond. He forced a smile and asked what he could do to help.

"Well, the hens have been fed, and the eggs collected," Mary said, "but you could weed the vegetable rows. You used to like doing that, remember?"

Ben nodded. It was best to be outdoors, keeping busy. But, as he stepped into the sunshine, he heard a shout. A short, stubby man in dusty clothes was striding towards the forge. The moment he saw Ben he halted and broke into a broad smile.

"So it's true!" he cried. "Master Mutton's come home!"

At once Ben smiled back, laughing at mention of the old nickname that had once irked him.

"Rattling Sam!"

"Who else could it be?" the other retorted. "Or has London dulled your eyesight, as well as your wits?"

He stretched out his hand and Ben went eagerly to take it. "Rattling Sam" Stubbs was the miller, whose creaky old windmill stood on the high ground south of the village, on a ridge known as the Hog's Back. Ben had known Sam all his life – and now realized how much he had missed him. He looked at the face, seamed with flour dust, under the familiar cap. Grey hair showed about Sam's ears now, while his black beard was flecked with silver. He peered closely at Ben, before letting go of his hand at last.

"Well...I can tell you've seen something of the world since I last set eyes on you," Sam said. "Done great things in the city, no doubt?" He grinned again. "You must come up to the mill and spin me your tales. I don't care if they're true or not. I get lonely up there with naught but the creak of machinery to listen to!"

"I will, gladly," Ben said.

He looked round as his mother came out of the forge. "It's rare to see you leave the mill, Sam," she said, with a polite nod. "Have you business in the village?"

At that Sam grew serious. "That I have, Mistress Mary," he answered. "Out at Justice Moon's. The fact is I'm on duty, in a manner of speaking..." He glanced at Ben.

"Sam's acting constable," Mother explained. "Though he's not been sworn in as such. No other man would take it on...too busy, they all said."

She smiled at Rattling Sam, and there was warmth in her eyes – a look of affection as well as respect. Of course Mary had known the man all her life too, but...Ben blinked: it seemed to him that her look spoke of more than just friendship. He glanced at Sam and this time he knew he was not mistaken. Whatever his mother's feelings were, Sam's were as plain as daylight. The miller had never married; he was wed to his work, he'd always said. But if ever a man looked heart-smitten, it was the one who stood here in the sunshine, gazing like a fool at Mistress Button.

And suddenly, as if realizing he had given himself away, Rattling Sam began talking quickly. "I'd have took the short cut along the Hog's Back to the justice's house, through the hayfields," he said. "Only I thought to come by here and greet you, young

Ben, seeing as you've been away so long – and anyway I need to speak to Parson Harrington, for 'tis a grave matter..."

He broke off and drew breath. "But maybe you've heard already," he said to Mary. "About the robbery?"

"No!" Mary exclaimed.

"A grave matter," Sam repeated. "A break-in, and a bit of damage done, Justice says. He sent his stable lad over a while back to tell me. But not much stolen, he said. That's something to be glad of, I suppose."

He hesitated. "Well, I've given you greeting, and I must go," he said to Ben, before turning to Mary "You'd better bolt your door at night. Of course the thief may be long gone, but you should be careful. And lock up the forge too, with the cow inside. Will you do that?"

"I will, Sam," she said. "And I thank you for stopping by."

Sam was about to go, whereupon Ben spoke up. "Can I come with you?" he asked. "As it happens, I've done a bit of investigating—" Then just in time, he stopped himself.

He had been about to speak of his adventures in London, when he had helped bring to justice some dangerous men: men as powerful as the Earl of

Horsham, or as ruthless as Sir Miles Brandon. But he realized he should not mention such matters. His mother knew nothing of the scrapes he had been in – let alone the times he had risked injury, even death. She would only worry about him, he thought. In fact, would she believe him? Some would not. Ben Button had always had a lively imagination, they would say, and must be exaggerating. He drew breath, and tried to sound casual.

"I mean – I'd like to help, Sam, if I can," he said. "I promise I'll do the weeding later, Mother. And I'd like to see Master Harrington again and..." He trailed off, seeing an uneasy look cross his mother's face.

But Sam grinned. "I don't see what harm it can do," he said. "Two heads are better than one – or I should say, two pairs of eyes, if there's looking around to be done!" He raised an eyebrow at Mary. "That is, if you've no objection?"

To Ben's relief, his mother shook her head. "It'll give him something to keep his mind busy," she said.

The two walked briskly through the street, and now Ben sensed excitement in the air. People were outdoors talking, and seeing Rattling Sam, some called out for news. But Sam did not stop, saying only that he was on his way to find out for himself.

"I didn't want to alarm your mother too much," he said, as they drew near to St Mary's church. "But it's not the first robbery I've heard of, these past days." When Ben turned sharply he went on: "A house down in Crux End, night before last…again someone forced a way in, but didn't take much." He shook his head. "A curious business. The news will spread soon enough, but keep it to yourself for now, will you?"

Ben promised he would and, all at once, a feeling of excitement stole over him too. It seemed as if there were a mystery – almost on his doorstep! He followed Sam through the wicket gate into the churchyard, to see a figure standing by the church door, with a hand raised in greeting.

Robert Harrington had been Hornsey's parson for the best part of thirty years. He had been Ben's teacher, as well as his mentor. Though he was a strict man, and Ben's memories of his teaching were not all happy ones, there was one thing he had never forgotten: it was Harrington who had given his blessing when John Symes came to ask Mary Button to let Ben join Lord Bonner's Men.

"Always remember, boy," he had said gravely, "that theatre began in the church. There's no shame in playing a part, so that people may see life acted out upon the stage. They may even learn from it!"

Those words had always stayed with Ben. It was the parson's voice he remembered best. He bowed low to Master Harrington – at which the man blinked in surprise.

"Is this Ben Button?" he exclaimed, squinting through his thick spectacles. "I heard you were home, but no one told me how you'd changed. Why, you're quite the young man!"

He turned to Rattling Sam. "Well, Stubbs, have you recruited this young fellow as your deputy?"

Sam was taken aback. "Nay, master, he asked if he could help. If you'd rather, I'll send him home…"

"Send him home? Certainly not!" The parson blinked, and adjusted his spectacles. "Master Button was my ablest pupil – the sharpest eyes and the sharpest wits, I always said. And it seems to me you could do with his eyes, since the justice's house is dark as a crypt… I take it that's where you're going?"

Sam nodded. "You've heard about the robbery, then?"

"I have… It troubles me greatly. And I've heard something else that troubles me more." Harrington sighed, letting his gaze stray beyond the quiet churchyard to the fields beyond.

"I know you will be discreet with these tidings," he said, turning to Ben. "Good Master Stubbs has enough on his shoulders already, yet the truth must out!"

He faced Sam, and his next words startled them both. "It's Daniel Cutter," he said. "I believe he's out of prison, and at large again."

Ben gave a start, while Sam stifled an oath before turning it into a cough. If every village had its bad penny, then Daniel Cutter was Hornsey's: a brawler and a thief, who was born to make trouble and had spent more time in the village stocks than anyone else alive. Ben remembered him well, though the young man had gone away long before Ben went to London. After Cutter left, unpleasant rumours soon reached Hornsey: he had been pilloried at Smithfield, it was said, for stealing a purse; and he had been in prison, where he was branded as a thief.

News of their son's misdeeds had come to Cutter's parents, two of the poorest people in Hornsey. Yet few condemned the couple, who had brought up their boy as well as they could. None knew why he turned out as he had: a stain on their name. Most folk said it was well that he had gone. If Daniel Cutter had returned to rob houses in his home village it would cause much distress. Why would he do that? Ben wondered.

"Nay – he'd never come back here!" Sam exclaimed. "It would be foolishness. A villain he may be, but Cutter's no fool, I'd swear to that."

"Most would echo your words, Sam Stubbs," the parson said quietly. "Yet a fox often returns to its kill, does it not?" He sighed. "I pray that I'm wrong...for the sake of the man's parents above all else. No one has suffered more for his crimes than they have!"

Sam seemed at a loss what to do. But Harrington put a hand on his shoulder. "Let us not leap to conclusions," he said kindly. "You must go to Justice Moon's and learn all you can. Tell him I stand ready to help in any way I might – as indeed does the whole village. I know Ben Button does..." A smile formed about his lips. "In fact, knowing our young friend as well as I do," he went on, "I dare say you'd be hard pressed to keep him away!

"You've taken no oath as constable," the parson went on. "I know you do it out of duty, rather than desire. So I hope Justice Moon does his duty as you have done, and appoints someone to the post officially. Perhaps now that he has become a victim of felony himself, he'll understand the urgency of the matter!"

Sam needed no further encouragement. With a grateful nod he turned and hurried back to the gate.

Ben was close on his heels.

But as he passed through, an odd thought struck Ben. These events may have brought trouble to Hornsey – but perhaps they were just what he needed to take his mind off his own worries. Eagerly he followed Sam out of the village. And his excitement only grew as the two of them walked uphill, towards the solitary house of Justice Richard Moon.

Chapter Five

*T*he justice's house turned out to be full of surprises.

Ben sidestepped the fallen tree, and followed Sam up the pathway. To his surprise the front door was open. Soon he was entering a gloomy hallway, where two people seemed to be shouting at each other.

"Stubbs, at last! Perhaps a cooler head will prevail, after all the fuss!"

The voice was high and crotchety. Stepping in from the sunlight, Ben narrowly avoided banging into Rattling Sam, who was making a clumsy bow.

The miller stood before a tall, thin man with a long, grey beard, who was dressed in a black, floor-length gown. A pair of blue eyes peered out from beneath a black skullcap. Justice Moon looked down at his first visitor, hardly noticing Ben. But when Ben made his bow – a more practised bow than Sam's – the man raised an eyebrow.

"Who are you? And what's your business?"

Quickly Ben gave his name. Then, as he was trying to think how to answer, Sam spoke up.

"Master Button's with me, sir," he said. "He has a sharp eye and a keen mind. The parson will vouch for him."

"Will he indeed?" the justice said, gazing stonily at Ben. There were other people in the hall: Ben recognized Hal Faraway, who was looking a lot less cocky than when he had last seen him. The other person was a stout woman in an apron and hood. When Ben caught her eye, she broke into a smile.

"Do ye not remember me? It's Doll Fisher, from Muswell."

At once Ben smiled back. He knew Dorothy Fisher, who had served the justice for years. She had grown plump, and her face was rather pale – but compared with the justice's it was almost sunburned. Master Moon looked like a man who rarely left the house –

which, most would have said, was true enough.

"It's Mary Button's boy," Doll said, turning to the justice. "Don't say you've forgotten him?" She threw a wry glance at Ben. "He'd forget to eat his meals, if I didn't stick 'em in front of him," she muttered. "Button – the blacksmith's son!" she shouted. "He went to London, remember?"

Ben was astonished: never in his life had he heard a servant address her master in such a fashion. But instead of chiding Doll for her insolence, the justice merely frowned and said: "The blacksmith's boy? Ah, yes! You've come to repair the damage. You'd better follow me. And you, Stubbs." Moon blinked, then noticed Hal, who was shifting his feet.

"What are you doing here?"

This time Ben almost gasped when Doll answered her master even more rudely. "Hal's been running messages for you all morning, you old fool!" she cried. "Let him get back to work, while you show Master Stubbs how we was broke into and robbed!" Throwing Sam a look of exasperation, she said: "There's little to see in any case. A window forced, but nothing took save an old sword." Hands on hips, she turned to the justice. "I'll return to the kitchen – unless there's aught else?"

She waited until the man shook his head.

Beckoning Ben and Sam to follow him, he shuffled across the hall to a closed door. As he opened it, Ben saw that the room was lit by candlelight...then he stepped over the threshold, and stopped in wonder.

He was in Justice Moon's laboratory.

The candles were lit because a heavy curtain over the high window blocked out the sunshine. In the yellow light Ben saw shelves from floor to ceiling, stuffed full of books and scrolls. Some had spilled onto the floor, which was in any case so cluttered it was hard to tell whether or not the room had been disturbed. A big table in the middle of the floor served as a desk, though it was almost hidden under a mass of books and papers. There were maps on one wall, and nearby on another table stood a dish of fruit: apples, pears, plums and dark cherries. But what caught Ben's eye was the globe. He had seen one only once before, in the house of his patron, Lord Bonner.

Sam stood by the desk, as if wondering what he could do here, when a sound startled them all: something between a squawk and a screech. It came from behind them. Ben looked round to see a large bird, bright green in colour, staring at him through the bars of a cage. As he stared back, the bird opened its beak – but what came out made Ben's jaw drop.

"When as the rye reach to the chin,
And chop-cherry, chop-cherry ripe within..."

"Be quiet!"

At Master Moon's shout the bird ceased its croaking rhyme. As if outraged at its owner, it made loud clucking noises before lapsing into silence.

"There's no need to look so alarmed. Have you never seen a parrot?" The justice gestured at his pet. "I purchased it at Billingsgate Dock. A seaman had brought it back from the Americas and I wanted to see if it could be taught to speak properly, as he claimed. Yet all it does is gabble nonsense like that!"

But Ben could hardly believe his own ears, for what he had heard was not nonsense. Not only did he recognize the words, they were from a play he knew as well as anyone in England – for he had once appeared in it and sung that very song!

"Excuse me, sir," he murmured, "but I know that air – 'Chop-cherry Ripe'. It's from a play called *The Old Wives' Tale*. I played Delia – I mean, I played a boy's part in it, at the Curtain Theatre."

"Indeed?" Moon put a hand to his great beard and tugged it. "Then I wonder how the creature comes to know it? Perhaps he learned the words from sailors."

Sam peered at the parrot as if it were bewitched. "Mercy, Master Justice," he muttered. "I know larks can sing, and I once heard of a jackdaw that could copy a man's speech. But 'tis not natural for a bird to speak rhymes like that!"

"It's only mimicry," Moon snorted. Moving to the table with the dish, he picked up a cherry and tossed it into the cage. At once the parrot hopped down from its perch and began pecking at the tasty-looking fruit.

"Animals imitate sounds all the time," he went on. "Not that I am expert in such matters. The stars and the planets are my field – and what a wondrous field that is! Why, the entire heavens lie open to any man who has the patience and the means to observe them—"

Abruptly he checked himself. "But see, we're not here to discuss my work," he muttered. To Ben's alarm, Moon suddenly rounded on him. "What did you mean, you've played at the Curtain Theatre?" he snapped. "I thought you were a blacksmith's boy, come to mend the window!"

Ben glanced at Sam. But Sam gave him a look which meant, *You'll have to talk your own way out of this*. So, drawing a breath, Ben gave a quick account of himself. He added that he was well known for "ferreting things out", and he would like to help investigate, if he could...

He trailed off, for the justice was frowning. Ben prepared for the worst: to be told to get out, and how dare he come here uninvited, a mere player-boy, and...

"Intriguing!"

Moon's frown was gone. To Ben's surprise, the man smiled at him!

"So you have an enquiring mind do you, Master Buttermilk?"

"It's Button, sir," Ben replied, "Er...I suppose I do."

"I'm glad to hear it," the justice said. "For the pursuit of knowledge is everything! I wonder Harrington did not recommend you to me. I could have used a boy like you over the years..." Then his smile vanished as quickly as it had appeared. It was hard to keep up with Justice Moon's thinking, Ben decided.

"I can't keep servants, you see!" Moon glared at Sam, as if it were somehow his fault. "Dolts, most of them! I had a boy serving me once who used a precious chart to light a fire! He couldn't understand what was on it..." He shook his head. "And the women come and go so often, I can hardly remember their names. Except Doll Fisher," he muttered, "though she only stays to annoy me!"

Sam cleared his throat. "Mistress Doll said a sword was stolen, sir," he murmured. "Is anything else missing?"

Moon tugged his beard again. "Not that I can see," he answered. "The sword was hanging on the wall. It hasn't been out of its scabbard in years. Otherwise..." The justice looked around. "Every corner, every shelf has been ransacked. It will take me days to go through everything." He sighed. "At least the upstairs room wasn't forced open."

"Upstairs room?" Sam echoed. "Are there valuables there?"

But the justice's manner changed again. Now he looked quite ferocious. "Never mind!" he cried. "If a locked room was untouched it's not your business, is it? Indeed, the rest of the house is none of your business. Here's where the villains got in, whoever they were, and here's where you may look – before you go and catch them!"

With sudden energy Master Moon strode to the window and threw back the curtain, making a cloud of dust. Sunlight flooded in through the grimy glass, along with a view of the backyard. But Ben's eyes went to the latticed window, and he saw that the justice was right. The latch had been forced open with a blade of some kind: there were scratches on the frame. It would have been a simple enough task for what folk in London called a *flick* or a *lifter* – a thief who knew his business.

But if Ben had been surprised earlier that the house of a justice could so easily be broken into, he was no longer. Master Moon was a most unlikely magistrate. He seemed to have no thought for anything apart from his studies...

"*Go away! You can't come in!*"

It was the parrot again. "Quiet, you wretch!" the justice cried, whereupon the bird made a loud, rasping squeal.

Moon turned to Sam. "Well, have you seen enough? I'd like to begin sorting my papers."

Sam did not reply. Instead he reached out and moved the window back and forth, causing its rusty hinge to squeak – and Ben gave a start. For the sound was exactly like that the parrot had made!

"Sir...your bird." He pointed. "You say it mimics things? It just mimicked the noise of the hinge opening! So, whoever got in here – it must have seen them, mustn't it? Perhaps there's some clue it can give us."

But to his disappointment Master Moon merely

snorted again. "Of course it would have seen them! What of it? Do you expect a description? This is a dull-witted creature; it can't talk, it merely copies sounds."

He began muttering into his beard, and Ben and Sam had to wait for him to finish. He must be a difficult master, Ben thought. He began to understand why Doll Fisher was so short-tempered, and why Hal had said that the justice did not like visitors.

"Forgive me, sir..." Sam drew himself to his full height, and looked Moon in the eye. "But I must remind you that I've not been sworn in as constable. I only stepped in because I'm...well, I'm a single man with no family, and everyone else hereabouts says they're too busy, and well...the matter is, sir, I don't know what I can do. A sword was stolen, and that's a felony right enough, but the man I should report it to is standing right in front of me! Apart from that, no money or plate or jewels was took, and your window only needs a repair to the latch. I don't mean by young Ben here," he added hastily, "for he's not prenticed to any blacksmith. But—"

Sam swallowed, realizing that he should watch his tongue. With an effort, he went on: "What's more, sir, whoever broke in did it at night, which means they'll be long gone by now. To London maybe, where you'd never find 'em in a month of Sundays. So, you being the justice, I'm reporting the crime, and while I think on it, another house was broke into, down at Crux End. So if you want my advice you'd best swear in a proper constable quick, for I never really wanted the job in the first place. There now – I'm done. And I ask your pardon for going on a bit, but it had to be said."

Sam let out a breath and waited, trying not to flinch under Moon's gaze. The justice appeared amazed at the miller's nerve. But Sam soon regretted his outburst, for the other announced: "Very well! Samuel Stubbs, I appoint you petty constable of this parish!"

And when Sam gulped, he went on: "You are sworn by ancient custom under common law, to prevent breaches of the peace, swearing, unlawful games, breaking of the Sabbath and eating meat on fast days. You are also to arrest rogues and vagabonds, organize the watch, and raise the hue and cry when needed. Your office is unpaid, though any charges from your duties will be borne by the parish. You will serve for one year. God save the Queen!"

Sam stood speechless. But having made his pronouncement, the justice clearly thought that was the end of the matter. "I shan't keep you any longer, master constable," he said. "If you wish to make enquiries of my servants, you have my permission. After that I leave you to carry out your investigation as you think best. Understood?"

Still Sam could not speak. Finally, with the briefest of nods to the justice, he went out through the doorway.

Ben followed, so taken aback himself that he forgot to make his bow. Nor did the two of them speak again until they had made their way by a stone-flagged passage to the kitchen. Doll Fisher looked up from a big table, where she was cutting up carrots and turnips.

"So," she said, "I see His Emptiness has dealt with you two as he deals with the rest of us. Will you take a bite of dinner?"

Chapter Six

*B*en and Sam were glad to accept Doll's offer of a bowl of pottage and a hunk of rye bread. They sat at the table, and Sam explained what had happened. But nothing Justice Moon did seemed to surprise Mistress Dorothy.

"So you're a real constable now," she said. She had finished the vegetables and was arranging a platter and mug on a tray. "That's a bind, isn't it?"

Sam was still trying to take it in. "Does your master not know I've a living to make?" he asked. "I've been grinding five hundred bushels of grain a week at the mill – six bushels an hour, when the wind's good and steady! How can I work if he expects me to go hunting for thieves – not to mention carrying out the other duties he's thrust upon me?"

"He don't consider anyone's feelings, he's that wrapped up in his books," Doll told him. "Why do you think I call him His Emptiness?"

She picked up the tray and carried it to the doorway. "I'll take his dinner in, then we'll talk if you want to," she said. "But there's little I can tell you, for I sleep soundly at night. I heard nothing save that mangy parrot!"

As she went out, Ben could not help but smile. The nickname "His Emptiness" may have been rude, but it was fitting in a way. Wiping his bowl with a piece of bread, he turned to Sam.

"I can help you look around," he said. "I could search for clues, while you carry on with your work. Then if I tell you where I've looked, you can let the justice think it's you who's been there."

Sam frowned at him. "That's a mite devious, Master Mutton." But a slow grin spread across his face. "Yet, it's a good plan – only, best not tell your mother, eh?"

* * *

After dinner the two of them made a search of the yard outside the laboratory window, but found nothing. The ground was too dry for footprints, and there were no other signs of an intruder. Nor was Hal Faraway any help. Although his bed in the stable loft was close by, like Doll, he said he had heard no noise in the night.

On the walk back to the village Ben and Sam were quiet, each busy with his own thoughts. Ben was thinking it was odd how the thief had stayed in one room, and not looked round the rest of the house for valuables. Stealing an old sword looked like an afterthought, hardly worth taking such risks for. And it seemed the door to the laboratory was not locked – nobody would go in there, Sam said, for people were afraid of the place. But mention of a locked upstairs room had caught Ben's imagination. He could not help wondering what was in that room. He was turning the matter over, when Sam jolted him out of his thoughts.

"I expect you know what's going on," he said, his eyes on the path. "With your mother and Dancer May, I mean."

Surprised, Ben gave a nod.

"I know times have been hard for her," Sam went on. "And since he's a man in need of a wife, I can

74

understand why Dancer's been round visiting and such..."

Glancing at his friend, Ben saw the same look in his eye that he had seen back at the forge. All at once, he had an idea what was coming next.

"The fact is, Master Mutton..." Sam tried to put on a jokey voice, but gave up. He stopped walking, and facing Ben he said: "The fact is, I worship the ground Mistress Mary walks on – always have. And if I thought she might come to see me as more than just an old friend, I'd fall on my knees and make her a proposal of marriage! There now – I've said it!"

"Then why didn't you speak to her before now?" Ben blurted out. "Instead of leaving it too late?"

"Well may you ask!" Sam shook his head. "I've been a coward and a dullard, that's why!"

Ben blinked. "You're no coward, Sam," he began, but the miller broke in impatiently.

"I am! I could have gone to her father long ago – when she was still young Mistress Jenkin, the ploughman's daughter. Only I was scared he'd turn me down – or worse, that she wouldn't want me. So I held off and your father asked her instead. He was a good man, Peter Button, and I knew he'd be a good husband..." Sam sighed. "To cut it short, Ben, I kept my own counsel. Since then I've watched you and

Edward and Margery grow up, and stayed a friend to your family, all the while fooling myself that that was enough. I had my mill to run, and—"

"You mean my mother is the reason you've never got married?" Ben broke in. "All this time—"

"All this time I've swooned over her, from that mill up on the Hog's Back," Sam finished. "Now – tell me I'm no coward!"

If only Sam had found the courage to court Mary, Ben thought, in the years after his father had died! Ben and Margery would have been glad to have Sam as their stepfather. Even Edward, he was sure. Was it really too late?

"I follow your thoughts, Ben," Sam said sadly. "If I'd been bolder, things might have turned out different. But after Christmas, Dancer got his feet under your mother's table, and next thing I know him and Edward are best of friends...and besides, he can provide a better home than I can. For apart from an old mill, and a hut that lets the wind through, what can I offer?"

"You've lots to offer, Sam!" Ben cried. "And anyway, only Edward really wants to live with Dancer, so—"

"Enough!" Sam looked embarrassed. "It's good of you to say that," he went on, "but I can't give you all a home. I'm at my work every waking hour, the mill creaks like it's falling to pieces when the wind's up, and my cottage is no better than a cowshed!" Sam laughed in spite of himself. "I could offer the cow a home," he said, "but what about the rest of you?"

Ben felt sorry for Sam, and disappointed for himself. If only there were a way to make his mother turn her attentions from Dancer...but he knew it was not so simple. People's feelings were complicated. In fact, just now, life at home looked more complicated than anything he had imagined.

"Cheer yourself, Master Mutton," Sam murmured. He tried to look his old self, but he did not fool Ben. "Perhaps I shouldn't have told you," he went on. "What's done is done, and I've no wish to go upsetting folk. Besides, since I'm constable now, I'll have enough to keep me busy. I'll barely have time to draw breath!"

He managed a grin. "Come on, we'd better get home. You've got vegetables to weed, and I've wheat to grind. So pick your feet up, eh?" And after clapping Ben on the shoulder, he set off at a good pace again.

Ben followed, his pace quickening, for a seed of hope had been planted in his heart: a hope that somehow, things might be turned about. He drew a breath as he strode alongside his friend, and soon the roofs of Hornsey's street came into sight again.

That afternoon, after finishing the weeding, Ben went down to the pasture with Margery to bring Eliza home for milking. As they walked he told her what Sam had confided to him. But he was surprised when his sister said: "I know, Ben. I guessed it a long time ago – and I think Mother knows too."

Turning to him, she went on: "She's never said anything about it, but you know she's no fool. She likes Sam. But even if she liked him enough to marry him…" Margery gave a sigh. "She's made up her mind that, out of necessity, joining our family with Dancer's is the best thing to do."

"Sam would be a much better husband," Ben said quietly. "And a good stepfather too."

"He would," Margery agreed sadly.

They crossed the Moselle Brook by the wooden bridge, and Ben found himself telling Margery about Justice Moon's laboratory, the parrot, and the thief who had taken nothing but an old sword.

Margery was uneasy. "They say Moon does magic there," she said, lowering her voice. "Alchemy, and drawing up strange charts. He has a stone that floats, and it always points to the north."

"I didn't see that," Ben said. "I was watching the parrot. It copies people's voices."

"You won't go back there, will you?" his sister asked. "They say the justice can put spells on people if they annoy him."

Since Ben did not really believe Margery's superstitions, he changed the subject and told her how he was looking for clues to the robbery. Though he was beginning to wonder if he had been rash in offering to help. As Sam had said, the thief, or thieves, would no doubt be far away by now, and if there were no signs outside the house, where else could he look? As Ben mulled this over he saw Margery smiling at him.

"You haven't changed a bit," she said. "You could never resist a mystery – something to puzzle over, until you'd found the answer!"

"In London some people call me *the ferret*," Ben said, smiling back. Margery laughed. Then all at once, a large brown bird flew over their heads. They looked round to see the bird swoop down and land on the outstretched arm of an old, sunburned man in a battered hat. The goshawk – for such it was, Ben realized – folded its wings and sat upright on the leather gauntlet the man wore. With a practised movement he pulled a little hood over the bird's head, then wound the thongs attached to its legs about his forearm. The hawk stayed still while its owner held it, looking at the Button children.

"It's Midge Martin!" Margery exclaimed. "I haven't seen him for weeks – come on!" And beckoning Ben to follow, she ran across the grass towards the old man.

Ben remembered Midge well. He had kept hawks all his life, and was an expert at tending them and doctoring them if they fell sick. Noblemen and wealthy merchants, who had built big houses up at Muswell and Highgate, often called on his services. All through his boyhood Ben had watched Midge exercising his birds. In fact it was hard to think of him without a bird on his arm, whatever the time of year.

As Ben and Margery drew close to Midge he returned their greetings, stroking the wing feathers of the goshawk with his fingers all the while. The bird was so still and quiet, it might have been a statue.

"Do you have a name for this one, Midge?" Margery asked, admiring the sleek hawk with its long pointed tail, its chest and legs covered with feathers of barred brown and beige.

"She's called Juno, young mistress," Midge said. "I raised her from an eyas...she's a fine hunter, and most clever. She has the keenest eyes of any hawk I've had!" Then as if to himself, he muttered: "Indeed, she's seen more than I'd care to think on, of late."

Ben wondered what he meant by that. He watched as Midge let Margery stroke Juno's wings. Then the old hawksman turned his gaze upon Ben. He was a man who knew a lot, some said, but usually he kept his thoughts to himself.

"Now I remember...," Midge narrowed his eyes. "You left home for the city, did you not, boy?" And when Ben nodded, he said: "Do red kites still perch on the rooftops in London, as I've heard – and soar about the Bridge Gate, pecking the flesh from traitors' heads?"

"They do, master," Ben admitted. "But I prefer not to watch them do it."

Midge wore a far-sighted look, as if he were always gazing at people from a distance. Perhaps it was because he spent so long staring at the sky, watching his hawks.

"'Tis a bird's nature to fly at carrion," he said. "It's food to them. Only men have the cruelty to put heads on pikes – indeed, to chop them off in the first place."

But Ben was still thinking over what the old man had said – about Juno seeing more than he liked to think on. Just then the goshawk made a slight movement on Midge's wrist. "She wants to go home," he said. There was a twinkle in his eye as he noticed Margery's disappointment.

"You'll see Juno again," he murmured. "Maybe I'll let you fly her one day. Would you like that?" Margery's face lit up. Midge nodded at her, then turned and walked off along the westward path to Muswell.

Ben and Margery crossed the pasture to where Eliza was tethered. Seeing them approach, the cow lifted her head and gave a loud bellow. "We're late for her milking, with talking to Midge," Margery said. "I hope Mother won't be angry." Picking up her skirts, she hurried across the grass.

Ben followed her, thinking about his mother and Dancer again – and about Rattling Sam too. Then, all at once, he remembered his visit to Granny Jenkin that morning. That was more urgent. He wanted to see Granny soon, and try to help her somehow. And by the time he and Margery returned home, leading Eliza, he had made a decision.

He would go back to his grandmother's cottage tomorrow. He would tell his mother in the morning.

And when he got to Granny's, this time he would stay until she let him in – even if he had to break the door down.

But the next day, when he awoke and found Edward already up and gone, everything changed. For no sooner had he come down the stairs than he heard voices, and saw people gathered outside in the street. His mother was there, talking with a neighbour. The moment she saw Ben she gestured for him to come out – and her words drove everything else from his mind.

"There's been another robbery," Mary said. "At Widow Luce's house by the church. The village is in uproar!"

Chapter Seven

Widow Luce was a severe woman, who rarely smiled. After her husband's death long ago in a time of plague, she had remained in their cottage by the church and devoted herself to hard work. She had no children of her own, but taught village girls the old skill of how to work flax and spin it into linen cloth. Despite her primness, people liked and respected her. So as soon as the news broke that she had been robbed, the folk of Hornsey hurried to her house to offer what help they could. By the time Ben and Mary Button arrived there was quite a crowd, outside as well as inside.

The break-in astounded Ben as much as it did anyone. It had happened during the night – the night after the robbery at Justice Moon's. Again, a back window had been forced open. And this time Ben sensed more than surprise at the event: there was fear, too. He saw it in the faces of those who stood about, talking among themselves. Now, it looked as if Sam had been wrong. For if it were the same thief who had broken into the justice's house, then perhaps he had not fled to London after all, but was still nearby!

Ben and his mother pushed their way into the cottage. Widow Luce sat by the chimney, sipping a cup of watered wine someone had brought her. Seeing Mary, she beckoned her to come close.

"I shan't be able to teach Margery today, mistress," she murmured. "I must collect myself."

"Mercy – don't think about that," Ben's mother said. "You've had a fearful shock. Was much taken?"

The widow shook her head. As her gaze fell upon Ben, she raised her eyebrows. Mistress Luce was one of those people who thought players were not respectable. Ben greeted her politely, though all he got in return was a stiff nod.

"One thing only was taken," the widow replied.

"Yet it causes me more pain than if I'd lost every penny I had." Turning to the chimney she pointed to a small space hollowed out between the bricks.

At that, one of the neighbours spoke up sadly. "It's the little beechwood casket that her late husband gave her when they married! Worth more to her than gold it was, and the thief stole it! Can you fathom such wickedness?"

"Was there money in it?" Mary asked.

Widow Luce shook her head. "No – just some old buttons. Nor had it a lock, so anyone could have opened the lid and seen for themselves..."

"Not in the dark, they couldn't."

Ben could not help speaking up. It didn't seem strange to him that the thief had simply taken the box, meaning to look inside it once he was away – especially if it held something that rattled. The break-in would have been in the dead of night, and no robber would risk a light. What seemed more strange was that nothing else was missing.

"Forgive me interrupting, mistress," he said, seeing Widow Luce's eyes on him.

The widow ignored him, and looked to those who stood near. "Well," she said, "in any case, I have a shrewd idea who it was took it: Daniel Cutter!"

A hush fell. Remembering what Parson Harrington

had told him, Ben realized that rumours were already flying about. Who else but Cutter, the village's "bad lot" who knew every house, would steal Widow Luce's casket? He might think there was money in it, or perhaps jewels...

"Yes, Cutter!" the neighbour cried. "What other man would be so bold, let alone so heartless? And likely it was he who burgled the justice. We've had no robbery in Hornsey for years. It must be him!"

Others were nodding. Outside the door, the name spread like a running flame: *Dan Cutter...a villain through and through... Cutter's come back to rob us!*

But something was amiss, Ben thought. On the face of it, Daniel Cutter seemed the most likely culprit. He would know about Widow Luce's casket, as he would know that there might be things worth stealing in the justice's laboratory. And there was the house down at Crux End. Ben knew little about that, but he recalled Sam's words: *someone forced a way in, but didn't take much...a curious business...*

It was indeed curious. Ben's mind went back to yesterday's visit to Moon's. He saw the justice in his black gown, telling him and Sam that every corner of the laboratory had been ransacked – and all at once an idea came to him.

Supposing these were not robberies at all? Or, at

least, not of the obvious kind... Might whoever was doing them be searching for something? Something worth taking risks for...something more valuable than an old sword, or the widow's casket? But then, what could Widow Luce's tiny cottage and Justice Moon's grand house have in common, he wondered, to tempt the thief?

There was a rising buzz of voices. Everyone was talking, except Ben's mother, who bent close to his ear.

"Whatever you're thinking," she murmured, "you'd better save it for Sam Stubbs."

As it happened, no one had yet gone to the mill to tell Sam about the robbery, so Ben volunteered to break the news.

The sun was climbing as he hurried through the village, passing the Bramble Bush, the old inn on the road out to Crux End. Once again he felt excited, as he left the path and veered south, where the ground rose to the Hog's Back. For not only could he take word to Sam, but he would also have the chance to tell him of his suspicions. Now he was keen to look for clues. He wanted to show those who thought badly of him – like Edward – that he was not just a foolish player who was good for nothing. And he realized something else: the one he wanted to convince most of all was Dancer May.

As he gained the higher ground, with the village behind him, Ben could see Dancer's farm to his left. He supposed Edward was there now. The hayfield was above the farm, while below it was green pasture where Dancer kept his cattle, fattening them for the London markets. Turning away, Ben strode to the windmill.

Sam's mill ground up wheat and rye nearly all year round. It was a small wooden hut, standing a few feet off the ground, suspended in mid-air on a big central post so that it could be turned to face the wind. Ben had been up the steps and inside the mill several times. It was a splendid sight on a windy day, with the creaking of cogwheels and millstone, the dust clouds and the soft hiss of the sails outside.

As he stood watching, Ben realized the sails were slowing to a halt. The long wooden pole, which acted as a brake, was being worked from the other side of the mill. The next moment Sam himself appeared round the corner in his dusty apron, and stopped in his tracks.

"Ben!" The miller smiled, then saw Ben's expression. "What's happened?" he asked.

Ben took a deep breath and told him.

By the time he had finished they were both sitting on the hillside looking down at the village. "So everyone's expecting me to go hunting for Dan Cutter now?" Sam sighed. "Even if I knew for sure it was him breaking into places, where would I look? He could be anywhere!"

Sam swept his hand sideways, to encompass the whole of Hornsey Vale, bathed in morning sunlight. Ben had to agree that it looked like a hopeless task. But since now seemed a good time, he voiced his suspicions that there might be more to this than just a series of burglaries.

To Ben's disappointment, Sam was not convinced. "What would a rogue like Cutter be searching for in a small village like ours?" he asked. "More like he broke into the justice's because it's the biggest house. And when he got only an old sword for his trouble, he decided to stay around and try his luck elsewhere." He frowned. "Funny thing is, if it was Cutter, surely he'd know Widow Luce hasn't got much money—"

"And what about the house in Crux End?" Ben broke in.

Sam shrugged and got to his feet. "Have you had breakfast?"

Ben shook his head.

"Then you'd best take bread and cheese with me."
Sam gestured to his little thatched house. Ben began
to follow him – then stopped suddenly.

"Why don't you appoint me under-constable?" he
asked.

Sam turned to him. "You're just a boy!"

"I'm almost a young man," Ben retorted. "You
heard the parson say it."

"Maybe so, but..." Sam scratched his head,
dislodging a small cloud of flour dust. "Your mother
would never allow it," he finished lamely.

"If I found something out that helped put an end
to the robberies she'd be proud of me," Ben said.
"And anyway, you're too busy to go hunting around
yourself."

"I'm not sure I've got the power to make deputies,"
Sam replied. "I'd have to ask the justice..." Then
seeing the disappointment on Ben's face, he sighed.
"But I suppose you could be a kind of *unofficial*
under-constable, if you like. Only, you must promise
you won't put yourself in danger. I remember Dan
Cutter as well as anyone – and he's not a man to
tangle with. Anything you find out, you come straight
to me with it. Do you swear to that?"

"I swear, master constable," Ben said. "Now, does
the offer of bread and cheese still stand?"

But an hour later, having breakfasted with Sam and then tramped round the village, Ben was feeling a lot less confident.

He had started by going back to Widow Luce's, to tell her he had reported the break-in to Sam. While he was there he managed to look at the back window, and saw it been forced open just as the one at Justice Moon's had. But when he tried asking questions, he got nowhere. Mistress Luce had been asleep in her bed and had heard nothing. Nor was anything else disturbed, as far as she could see. She only knew someone had been in the house when she saw the empty recess in the chimney, where her casket always rested. Speaking of that upset her, she said, and anyway, didn't Ben have things to do?

So he had taken his leave, but instead of going home he had slipped round the back of the cottage and poked around. But as at the justice's, all he had found was a patch of flattened grass beneath the window. And since he already knew the thief had got in that way, it did not help him much.

With the sun high overhead, Ben widened his search. From the Bramble Bush at the western end of the village to St Mary's Church at the eastern end he walked, peering in back gardens, and peeping into outhouses when no one was looking. But he saw nothing untoward. Finally he worked his way northeast, crossing the path to Tottenham Wood, where he had been the morning before to visit Granny Jenkin's. He remembered his resolve to go back to Granny's. But walking the fields north of the village, he thought it best to let his mother know first. Soon he was clambering over the garden wall, to find Margery feeding the hens. But instead of smiling, she greeted Ben with a glum face.

"Mother's not here. She's left chores for me, and gone up to Dancer's." She looked uncomfortable. "You should go there too, since you look like you're at a loose end."

Ben watched her throw down the rest of the scraps, then said: "I told you, I'm helping Sam look for clues to the robberies."

To his surprise, his sister rounded on him. "Are you indeed!" she cried. "What about us – your family?"

"How do you mean?" Ben asked, taken aback. "If you're thinking of Dancer—"

"I don't mean him," Margery answered. "I mean Mother and me! We've hardly had time for a proper talk with you yet. You and Edward have fallen out already, and Mother's sad you don't want her to marry Dancer, and..." She broke off, seeing Ben looking unhappy.

"I'm sorry," she muttered. "I know you don't mean any harm." She sighed. "I'm worried about Granny. I only hope Dancer will agree to give her a home. What's going to happen to her otherwise?"

That was all Ben needed to make his mind up. "Well, the first thing that's going to happen is I'm going to see her right now," he said. "And this time I'm not leaving until I've spoken to her!"

At last, Margery brightened. "Good," she said. "And I'm coming with you!"

Chapter Eight

*B*en and Margery walked up the Tottenham path, and after a while they talked about Widow Luce and her missing casket.

"Isaac Cutter's upset at talk of his son being the thief," Margery said. "He swears he hasn't set eyes on Daniel since he went to London, and that's years ago. He says he's nothing to hide, and anyone can search his cottage – not that anyone will. They believe him."

Thinking of Daniel Cutter made Ben angry for the distress the man had caused to his parents, and to the whole village. People were nervous, wondering whose house might be next, though it wasn't as if any of them had much to steal. Once again he began puzzling over whether Cutter really was the robber. He was wondering whether to tell Margery his own suspicions when Granny Jenkin's cottage came into view.

All looked peaceful, as it had been on Ben's visit the day before. But as they walked round to the garden, both of them grew uneasy. They stopped, gazing at the door.

"Granny always keeps it open in summer," Margery said.

Taking a breath, Ben marched up and rapped loudly on the door. "Granny!" he shouted. "It's Ben. I'm back!"

Margery walked up to the door too. There was no answer, so Ben knocked again, louder this time. Then he thumped the door, so hard that it shook. But still there was no sound.

"Granny!" Margery called. "Mother's worried about you. She's coming herself, soon. If you're there, why don't you let us in?"

"I'm certain she's there," Ben said. "Like she was yesterday." Again he banged on the door – and now a noise came from inside the house. It sounded like someone falling over.

"Granny!" Alarmed, Ben turned the iron handle,

but the door wouldn't open. He pushed harder, then threw his weight against it. "I think it's wedged shut," he said.

"Something bad's happened to her!" Margery cried. "We'll have to try the windows..."

"They're shuttered." Ben pointed – then both of them started. At last the door had opened, but only a few inches.

"Go away, you fools!" a voice yelled. "Leave me alone!"

"Granny!" Margery cried. "It's me and Ben—"

"I know who you are!" Granny shouted. "Do you think I'm moonstruck? Get you gone!"

They could see her now. There was no mistaking their white-haired grandmother, in her old frock and apron. With one gnarled hand she gripped the edge of the door. The other she held to her throat, almost as if she were in fear of her own grandchildren.

"Please let us in, Granny," Ben said. "Everyone's worrying about you. They're saying—"

"I don't care what they're saying!" Granny retorted. "I'm right as rain. Tell your mother not to come. I don't want anyone here!"

Ben tried to look his grandmother in the eye, to see if her old spark was still there. He would know if she was not herself. But she refused to look at him, which was not like Granny. Gingerly he reached forward but, to his dismay, she slapped his hand.

"Are you deaf?" she cried. "I told you to go. What don't you understand?"

Beside him he heard Margery gasp. This was not the grandmother they knew... But then he too caught his breath. For Granny had looked straight at him – so briefly that most people would have missed it. But in that second, Ben read something that made his heart jump: Granny wasn't confused – she was terrified!

And at once, he knew he must do what she wanted. Sensing Margery was about to speak, he grabbed his sister's arm to silence her.

"Very well, Granny," Ben breathed. Suddenly, he was acting! "I'm sorry we bothered you," he said, in a loud voice that took Margery by surprise. "I'll tell Mother you want to be left alone, and you'll come to the village when you're ready. Does that please you?"

Granny let out a sigh, and Ben knew his instincts had been right. The old woman sagged, as if she had been holding her breath. "It pleases me well," she said at last. "There's nothing amiss, and naught for folk to worry about. You may go back – and forgive me for slapping you."

Ben nodded stiffly, though his heart was racing. He knew he was not mistaken: Granny was pretending, just as he had, though – unlike Ben – she was no player, and her voice sounded unnatural. Ben knew that she was forcing herself to say things she did not mean. And he had guessed something else, something terrible: there was someone in the cottage with her, watching them!

"It's nothing," Ben answered, keeping his voice steady. "We'll go now. Look after yourself, Granny…" He signalled to Margery that they must leave. As he turned, however, he leaned towards the old woman, meaning to mutter something, just to let her know he understood. But instead, it was Granny who spoke to him, though what she said made no sense:

"*The Black Onion!*" she whispered. "*The Black Onion!*"

Then she stepped back and slammed the door. There was a sound as if something was being shoved against it, then silence.

And all Ben could do was grip Margery's hand and pull her away, back towards the woodland path.

That afternoon there was a family gathering in the last place Ben wanted to be: the kitchen of Dancer's farmhouse. But since his mother had been out when he and Margery had reached home, Ben had left his sister and hurried up the Hog's Back, for the second time that day. First he'd gone to Sam's mill and told him what had happened. Which meant that Sam, who no more wanted to be at Dancer's than Ben did, had felt obliged, as constable, to come along.

At first no one wanted to believe Ben's tale about an intruder at Granny's. They stood round looking uneasy – especially Sam, who stayed near the door. Mary Button found herself between Sam and Dancer, who each behaved as if the other wasn't there. But they all knew Ben was a truthful boy, just as they knew how oddly Granny Jenkin had been acting lately. When he repeated the words Granny had whispered to him, however, there was a puzzled look on every face.

"*Black Onion?*" Dancer gave a snort. "There's no such thing! I've farmed all my life, and I never heard of it!"

"Nor me," Sam admitted. "But I'm more troubled about this notion that there was someone else in the cottage." He looked at Ben. "You really think your grandmother was being forced to send you away?"

"Yes!" Ben nodded firmly. On his way to Dancer's he had become more convinced than ever that Granny was in fear of her life. Again he described how she had pretended that nothing was wrong, and she simply didn't want visitors. But he knew she was trying to tell him she didn't mean it. And why were the windows closed up, and the door wedged shut? To Ben, his was the only explanation that made sense.

Mary was very worried. "Well, I'm going to Granny's," she said. "I won't rest until I've found out what's going on!" She looked at Dancer as if expecting him to say he would go with her. But Dancer kept quiet, looking rather uncomfortable.

Just then there was a sound at the doorway, and Edward came in. With him was a fair young woman whom Ben had not yet seen since his return: Dancer's daughter, Ellen May.

"So it *was* you I saw, Ben." Ellen smiled at him. "Your brother said you'd changed, but you look the same to me. Just a couple of inches taller."

Ben greeted her. He had no ill feeling towards Ellen. She was a hard-working country girl, with none of her father's bombast.

"Have you not offered our guests a drink, on such a hot day?" she asked Dancer. But Mary spoke up quickly.

"We must go, Ellen. Dancer will tell you why..."

She paused. "Unless he wants to accompany me?"

Dancer cleared his throat. "I would – gladly," he answered. "Only…well, the matter is—"

"There's no need." Sam spoke up quietly. "I'm constable, so I'll go."

There was a moment's silence, but Ben saw the look Dancer threw at Sam. He knew that expression, for he had watched Hugh Cotton play the role of a jealous lover. It seemed strange, and rather alarming, to think that his mother was the cause of rivalry between men like Dancer and Sam. Fortunately he knew neither of them was likely to challenge the other to a duel, as gallants did in plays.

"Thank you, Sam," Mary said. She looked hurt. Turning away from Dancer, she faced Edward. "Ben can come with us, but you'd better go home. Margery's on her own, and—"

"I've got things to do," Edward said, with a scowl. "I only came in to see what all the fuss was about—"

"There's no fuss," his mother said sharply. "And don't answer me back!"

Sam, who had stood aside when Edward and Ellen came in, moved to the doorway. "Let's be off shall we, mistress?" he said. To Edward, he added: "We're concerned about Granny Jenkin, son. Everyone's a mite edgy, with what's happened lately. I mean, all the talk of Dan Cutter hiding out somewhere, and…"

With a gasp, he broke off.

Ben was staring at him. "You don't think…?" he began – whereupon the others stiffened. Ellen drew a sharp breath.

"No – it couldn't be!" Sam muttered, then he gulped. "Could it?"

Mary's hand flew to her mouth.

"I mean could Cutter be hiding out at Granny's, while he goes out by night to rob?" The miller shook his head. "Surely even he wouldn't be so cruel as to force her to shelter him…would he?"

But, for Ben, there was no more time to lose. "Let's get over there, quick!" he cried.

"Wait!" Sam raised his hand. "We could be wrong…"

"What if we're not?" Mary was already at the door, but she paused to snap an order that made Edward jump. "Home – now!" she cried. "And stay with your sister until I get back!"

Without a word the boy turned and went out of the doorway. Mary, Sam and Ben followed him. Then as Edward ran off downhill towards the village, the other three started in another direction: towards Tottenham Wood.

* * *

By the time they reached the Tottenham path, Sam and Mary were out of breath. Ben, who was fleet-footed, could easily have outrun them, but had to let them keep up. Their slower pace had one good result, however: it brought some help. As they hurried on, they came across a young man named Roger Graves, a farmer's boy. Startled by folk who appeared so agitated, he asked what the trouble was. Sam paused to gasp a few words of explanation, but it was enough. Like everyone in the village, Roger knew Granny Jenkin well and would have done anything to help her. Soon not three but four people were hurrying into the wood.

Nothing was said until the old ploughman's cottage came into view. Once again, all looked quiet to Ben. But as the others slowed down, he and his mother increased their stride. With Ben close behind, Mary ran round the corner of the house, crying out: "Mother, it's me!"

Then both of them stumbled to a halt – for the door was wide open. Ben's heart sank as he thought the very worst.

"Granny!" he shouted. "Are you there?"

Sam Stubbs and Roger Graves hurried up behind.

"Wait!" Sam called breathlessly. "Better let me go first..."

But Ben ignored him, and so did Mary. The two of them hurried forward, only to be stopped by a piercing cry. The next moment, a white-haired figure in an old apron appeared in the doorway, hands outstretched towards them.

And as everyone cried out in relief, Granny Jenkin tottered the few yards from her doorway to fall into her daughter's arms. Soon Mary Button was shedding tears, as she hugged the frail figure to her chest.

But Ben, though he felt relieved too, let his gaze wander towards the cottage. And when Rattling Sam and Roger Graves went to the doorway, he followed them inside – only to halt at the fearful sight.

His first thought was that Granny had been burgled, just as Justice Moon and Widow Luce had. The cottage was a mess: a chair overturned, crockery smashed, even shelves were broken. The shutters that had been closed were torn down, and one window was completely shattered. The floor was strewn with broken pots and jars, their contents crushed as if by heavy feet: the fruits of Granny's work, ruined. Ben's mood went quickly from one of elation at finding Granny safe, to dismay at what he now saw.

The three of them stood in silence, until finally Sam turned to leave, and Roger went with him. Ben wrenched his eyes away from the scene and followed the others outside...to receive another shock.

Granny was still being comforted by his mother. But now she turned with a wild look in her eye, and pointed a shaking hand at the cottage.

"He's gone!" she cried. "Gone at last, since the other one came for him – just like he feared – not half an hour ago!"

Ben, Sam and Roger gathered about the two women. "Who's gone, Mother?" Mary asked, perplexed.

"Dan Cutter!" Granny cried. "He fought hard, but he was taken just the same... You must find him soon," she said, to no one in particular. "Or heaven knows what will happen!"

Then she let out a long sigh. "It was all because of the Black Onion," she muttered. "I wish I'd never heard of it!"

Chapter Nine

By the time Ben and his mother brought Granny back to the village it was evening. Roger Graves went home, saying he would spread the word about what had happened. But Sam came to the Buttons' cottage and sat at the table to hear the old woman's account of her ordeal. For, unknown to everyone, an ordeal was what poor Granny had been suffering, alone, for almost a week.

At first she seemed confused and kept wanting to go back to her cottage, until Mary persuaded her to remain. Sam helped, telling Granny that he would go there with others soon, and put the place in order. There was no serious damage, he told her, putting on a cheerful face – nothing that a few willing men couldn't repair. It wasn't as if her house had been set on fire, he added. But at once Granny let out a whimper.

"That's what he said he'd do, if I didn't hide him!" she cried. "Burn it down – not my house, but *this* house, with all of you inside it! That's why I had to help him!" She turned to Ben. "It's a good thing my clever grandson knew something was wrong," she went on. "For Dan Cutter was behind the door – not six feet away from you, listening to every word! He told me to get rid of my visitors, or things'd get worse, not just for me, but for you too!"

Everyone was shocked. The children sat round the table, with bowls of warmed-up pottage for a hasty supper, though they had eaten little of it. Edward was subdued, while Ben and Margery exchanged looks. Sam, however, kept his eyes on the old woman.

"Calm yourself, mistress," he said kindly. "No one's going to burn anywhere down. Cutter's gone now." He frowned. "Though I'd like to know who this other fellow is that you spoke of."

"Him!" Granny drew a sharp breath. "Don't speak of him…" Seizing the mug of warm ale that Mary had poured, she took a thirsty gulp. "Dan Cutter's a rogue," she went on, "though he's no murderer. But the other one..." She gave a shake of her head. "It was him Cutter was hiding from, don't you see?"

Suddenly Ben's mind was busy. This other man – the one who had fought with Daniel Cutter and taken him away by force – might this be the real thief, the one who had scared the whole village? He was eager to ask questions of Granny, but he knew he must tread carefully.

"Why don't you tell me how it all started?" Sam asked. He put out his hand and took hold of Granny's. The old woman did not resist, but let her hand rest in Sam's for a moment, before letting out a long sigh.

"I only know what Cutter told me, Master Stubbs," she said wearily, "and that wasn't much. How it started I can't say – but I know *where* it started: in Newgate Prison!"

And at last, with everyone hanging on her words, Granny told her tale.

"They were in jail together," she began. "Dan Cutter for stealing, until he was branded." She held up her hand, with the thumb extended. "He's got a 'T' burned here, for 'thief'. But the other one..." She shuddered. "The other was in Newgate for worse: murder! He killed a man in a fight, Cutter said, and should have hung, but he got off, free as a bird! Can you believe that?"

"How can that be?" Sam asked.

"He pleaded his neck verse!" Granny told him. "All he had to do was read out a psalm, Cutter said, and they let him off with a flogging – because he's an educated man. Benefit of clergy, they call it."

"Well now, I believe I've heard of such," Sam said thoughtfully. "It's an old law, that dates from when a man who could read was likely to be a priest, and could escape execution. A gentleman can still get away with it, even though he's no priest, just by proving he can read – and likely slipping the jailers a bribe, too."

He turned back to Granny. "That's grave news, mistress," he muttered. "For this one sounds like a mighty dangerous fellow. Did Cutter speak his name?"

Granny shook her head. "No name," she said. "No face, either. I never saw him, but I felt him. Like a bad spirit! I ran upstairs when he broke in!"

Suddenly she looked as terrified as when they had found her at the cottage. "And I heard him," she went on. "Heard them arguing, heard his voice..." She lowered her eyes. "Best part of six days, Cutter was under my roof – scared stiff the whole time. He said someone was after him, and he wouldn't hurt me so long as I let him stay, and fed him. Then today – soon after Ben and Margery had gone – the other one came, bold as brass. Smashed the window and the shutters in, easy as snapping a twig!"

Granny shuddered again. "The strange thing was, he was so well spoken," she said. "After things went quiet – why, he even sang as he took Cutter away. I heard him!" She began humming to herself. And as everyone stared, she broke into a song that made the hairs on the back of Ben's neck stand up:

"When as the rye reach to the chin,

And chop-cherry, chop-cherry ripe within..."

The old woman stopped and sighed. "I must sleep," she said. "I'm that tired, I don't know what I'm saying."

She yawned, and Mary got up to help her to her feet. But Ben could not wait. "You heard him sing that song?" he asked. "Are you certain?"

"Certain?" Granny murmured. "Of course I am..."

"There's something you haven't told us, Granny," Ben went on urgently. "The Black Onion – what is it?"

But Granny's answer came as a disappointment. "I don't know, but that's what they were fighting about. It must be mighty important...though who ever heard of a black onion?"

She gave another yawn, and Mary took her off to bed.

Soon after that, Ben seized the opportunity to speak to Sam alone. "That song that Granny heard – it's the same one—"

"Aye – the one Moon's parrot recited," Sam finished, with a frown. "I scarce know what to make of it."

But Ben did. "It was him!" he said excitedly. "Not Cutter – he never left Granny's. It was the other man who broke into the justice's. He must have been singing that song to himself while he searched the laboratory – how else would the parrot have picked it up?"

Sam's frown deepened. "Well – if you're right," he said, "he must be a very cool-headed thief indeed."

The next day was the Sabbath, but it was no ordinary Sunday morning. St Mary's church was crammed to the door, as the village assembled to hear Parson Harrington. Rumours were all over Hornsey, after Roger Graves had brought the news that Granny Jenkin had been held prisoner in her own home. But it was her account of Daniel Cutter's flight – or rather, his being taken away by an unknown man, who sounded even more dangerous – that caused real alarm. Already people were talking about forming an armed group to search around the village. Among these was Dancer May, who sat next to Mary Button on the end of a pew, where the family were squashed together.

"Stubbs isn't up to this task," Dancer growled. "We should go to the justice and demand he appoints someone else – someone with more wits!"

Ben sighed. He was tired of Dancer sounding off: he knew the real reason the man disliked Sam, but he didn't want to think about that now. His mind was still preoccupied with yesterday's events – especially the Black Onion. He had thought of little else since he woke up. The more he pondered it, the more it intrigued him. What on earth could it be?

A hush fell as Parson Harrington came in to take the service. He behaved as if all was normal, though he was aware that folk were on edge, waiting for a pronouncement. The moment came after the last hymn was sung, and a silence fell.

"I have grave tidings for you all," the parson said. "Words I never thought to utter in my long years serving our community. But you have heard the rumours, so I will not mince my words: a dangerous felon is at large – and may still be within our parish. Indeed, it may be not one man, but two, who must be sought. So we should all be vigilant, and look out for one another. I'm here to give what help I can, as is the justice, I'm certain," he went on. "I will speak with him today, so we may decide on the best course of action."

At that a muttering began, until the parson cleared his throat loudly. He looked to Rattling Sam, who was sitting across the aisle from Ben's family. "Now I call upon our constable to address you," he said.

Sam rose to face the congregation. There was a snort from Dancer, but Sam pretended he had not heard. "My friends," he began, "you've heard our parson and you've heard the news. What with this revelation, and the break-ins, we must pull together. I don't just mean barring doors, keeping a watch on our own houses and such, but looking out for neighbours too. Maybe you can offer a bed to one of the old folk, until this business is over. Those who live alone might share their homes..." Sam hesitated, but there were no objections. He went on: "I'm asking all able-bodied men and older boys to form a watch, to patrol the village day and night. Two parties taking turns is best. Anything suspicious, don't be afraid to report it.

Meanwhile I'll speak with the justice too, see what can be done…"

Once again, there was muttering. *Justice won't do anything…he never does…*

"Now, let's not work ourselves into a sweat," Sam said, raising his voice. "Rest assured I won't stop until we've dealt with this danger. Not until we've caught the man, or men, and turned them over to the law – or satisfied ourselves they've fled. And by 'law', I mean someone higher up than myself," he added, causing some laughter. "So will you help me?"

There was a chorus of agreement, at which Sam looked relieved. Even Dancer muttered "Aye", along with the others. But the next moment there was surprise, as an old man in black clothes stood up at the back of the church, and spoke in a shaky voice.

"I'll be joining you too, Master Stubbs. And you'd best not try to stop me, for I've as much right as anyone here!"

It was Isaac Cutter. Ben watched with everyone else as the father of Daniel Cutter walked slowly up to Sam. A hush fell as he turned to face the village.

"Like our parson, and Sam too, I won't mince words," Isaac said. "I know what my son's done, and I'm racked with shame because of it. I can't blame you for wanting him punished – but I know other things too. I know he wouldn't steal from any of you, or harm the folk he grew up with and has known all his life. Nor would he have forced an old woman to shelter him if he hadn't been frightened for his own life! And more, I..."

He trailed off as voices rose. There was some sympathy for Isaac, but there was also anger. The village was not in a forgiving mood, and Master Cutter sensed it.

"And another thing I know!" he went on. "I tell you, my son's not a cruel man – only desperate! Whatever he did in London, he's paid the price for it – and I still have hope that he may see sense one day, and change his ways. So let me say this: Dan's not the villain who broke into Widow Luce's house, nor the justice's! I would swear to it. This other man is the one we must seek – though there's no doubt Dan's involved, and my boy's got some explaining to do! That's why I'm joining the watch, to see justice done. I ask you to let me stand with you!"

The old man turned to Sam. And putting a hand on Isaac's shoulder, Sam spoke to the congregation again. "I've naught to add to that," he said. "Nor have I any objection. Has anyone?" He threw a glance at Dancer, who looked away. Ben's heart was warmed as, following Sam's example, people relented.

Now Parson Harrington stepped forward. "I say 'Amen'," he intoned, in his best pulpit voice. "And if there's nothing further, the service is over." He turned to leave through the vestry door. And, soon after, the population of Hornsey got to their feet and went out into the sunshine.

Ben was among the last to emerge, with his mother, Edward and Margery. Granny was asleep when they had left the house, and Mary was anxious to get home. To Ben's surprise she did not wait for Dancer, but started off at once with Margery.

Edward, of course, stayed behind. "Able-bodied men and boys are wanted," he said to Ben. "Perhaps you'd best go back with Mother."

"I've promised to help Sam," Ben replied, looking round. Already men were assembling, talking among themselves.

"What do you think you can do?" Edward asked, allowing a sneer to creep into his voice. "This is real danger – not play-acting!" But just then Sam came out of the church. The other men gathered round him, so Ben and Edward went to join them.

"Farmer May has agreed to lead the daylight watch party," Sam was saying. "They'll start at the church at midday and circle the village, ending up back here by evening. I'll take the night party, starting out at sunset." He looked round at the other men.

"I ask all of you to arm yourselves," he said quietly. "I know none of you has sword or pistol, and I don't suppose many of you have daggers – a stout stick or a cudgel will serve. Even a rolling pin, if you prefer."

There were a few smiles, but no one spoke. There was no doubt that they might face danger, now that Granny's tale was known. The men began to form two groups. Those with young families preferred to be at home after dark, so joined the first party, while older men joined the night watch. Several boys clamoured to go with the later group, only to be disappointed when Sam told them to join Dancer's party. But none was as angry as Edward, once he learned Ben was to go with Sam's group.

"It's not right!" he cried. "Since Ben's the eldest, and we've no man at home, he should stay and look after Mother and Margery. I can wield a cudgel or a sling-stone, I know every hillock and every tree, and—"

Sam raised a calming hand. "It's because you've no man at home that I want you to guard your mother and sister tonight – and your grandmother too," he said. "I need a brave fellow, one I can rely on for that. So – what do you say?"

Edward scowled, but since everyone was looking at him, he gave a nod.

"Then it's settled," Sam said. "Now I'm for home – my mill won't run itself. I'll see you men at sunset."

He said farewell to the watchmen but, with a look, he let Ben know that he wanted him to follow. So after waiting until people had dispersed, Ben ran and caught up with him.

"Thank you for letting me come, Sam," he began – but the miller turned to him with a grave expression.

"I didn't do it as a favour, Ben," he replied. "I need your wits, and your keen ears." He sighed. "If your mother's worried about you coming along tonight, tell her I'll keep an eye on you. Now, you'd best go home."

With a nod, Ben took his leave. He could hardly wait until nightfall. And if he felt a little scared, his nervousness was tempered by excitement.

For he knew, without any doubt, that he was about to plunge deeper into the mystery.

Chapter Ten

The daylight search of Hornsey village and the surrounding fields turned up nothing. All afternoon Dancer's party tramped about, poking under hedges and looking in huts and barns, as Ben had done the day before. But they found only an empty purse someone had dropped outside the Bramble Bush. By evening, weary and footsore, the group broke up and went home. But then, some muttered, what had they expected to find? Surely a thief who managed to rob places without anyone setting eyes on him would keep well hidden? And in any case, who was to say he hadn't already gone, and Dan Cutter too?

The second party gathered at sunset, Ben and Roger Graves among them. Each man had armed himself, some with cudgels, others with billhooks or hatchets. A few had torches to light against the dark, and Roger had brought his dog Gimlet. Gimlet had a good nose for danger, he said, though Ben guessed he was there more to keep his master company than for any other reason.

Last to arrive was Isaac Cutter. He was somewhat out of breath, but insisted he would not slow the party down. So without delay they followed Sam out of the churchyard, crossed the Tottenham path and began walking the fields north of the village.

At first nobody said much. But when someone asked Sam if he had spoken to the justice, the miller looked glum.

"Parson and I went to see him this afternoon," he answered. "But all he said was that his task is to pass sentence on felons, not catch 'em. Then he gave me a lecture on my duties – and you know what else? He said as he's the most important man round here, we should place watchmen at his house until the thieves are caught!" Sam tapped the billet he had fixed to his belt. "I don't mind admitting what I felt like doing after that."

There were a few smiles, and the men began to relax. They were an armed group, perhaps a dozen in number, and however dangerous their foe might be, he could hardly overpower them. Conversation began, but since it was mostly gossip, Ben grew bored with it. When he had left the forge he was excited, and proud to be part of the village watch. Now, it looked as if the night search would prove as fruitless as the daylight one.

But after half an hour, as the sun was disappearing behind Muswell Hill, someone appeared out of the gloom, bringing the party to a startled halt.

"Midge Martin, is that you?" Sam peered ahead, as the familiar figure approached. As usual, a hooded hawk was perched on his wrist.

"It is, Master Stubbs." Midge surveyed the ragtag body of men without expression. His eyes fell on Ben, the youngest one present, before settling on Sam.

"I heard you needed help," Midge said, stroking the bird's feathers as he spoke. Ben was sure it was Juno the goshawk again. "And seeing as a hawk's eyes are best," he added, "I thought I'd have a walk around, before it got too dark."

Midge wore his far-off look. "I confess I've been uneasy of late," he went on. "Or I should say, my hawks have."

The party were gathering round. "Do you know something, Midge?" Roger Graves asked. Beside him, Gimlet was watching the goshawk. The old man looked to see that the dog was held firmly on its leash, before giving his answer.

"The birds do," he replied. "But I can't say what." He nodded towards the east, where Tottenham Wood was lost in the dusk.

"I didn't want to cry wolf," he went on. "No sense scaring folk without reason. Only, there's been something…" He fixed his gaze on Sam. "…Some*one*, I should say, moving about, fast as a flittermouse." He paused. "A dangerous fellow – evil. I know no other word for such as he."

There was an intake of breath from the watchmen. "Then I'd be glad if you'd tell us what you know," Sam said urgently. "And there's a lot of frightened people in the village would be glad of it too."

But Midge would not be hurried. "The hawks have been edgy, these past days," he said. "There's been times they weren't keen to hunt…or places they didn't want to linger." Once again, the old man jerked his head towards the east. "Every time it's over there towards the Heights. So today I had a walk in the woods myself, to see what I could find." He shrugged. "I was too late. That particular bird has flown."

The other men were exchanging looks, when all of a sudden someone pushed through them to stand before Midge.

"If you mean my son, why don't you say so!" Isaac Cutter cried. "But he's no more evil than you are!"

"I didn't say it was Daniel." Midge faced the other man. "I've heard the talk, but I'd say this fellow's a stranger, who doesn't know the country." He glanced at his goshawk, which had flinched. "She don't like raised voices," Midge went on, with a frown at Isaac. "That's why I steer clear of folk."

He looked at Sam. "I found no one in the woods," he said. "But someone's been there – look for yourselves." And eager to be off, the hawksman turned away.

"Wait!" Sam called. "Can't you tell us more? Are there signs someone's been hiding?"

Midge was murmuring softly to his hawk. Without looking up, he said: "You know the old hornbeam, that was struck by lightning?"

Sam said that he did. The huge tree was a landmark deep in the wood that was familiar to Hornsey folk. It had been split long ago during a storm.

"Walk south from there," Midge told him. "You'll see a fallen oak. A space has been hollowed out beneath it."

"You said there was someone moving like a flittermouse," Isaac Cutter broke in. "Did you not see him?"

"Shadows," Midge muttered. "I saw no one clearly…" He hesitated. "Heard something, though, a few nights back. "'Twas so strange, I thought my ears were playing tricks – it sounded like someone was singing."

Ben drew a sharp breath, but Sam grew brisk. "I thank you," he said to Midge. "We'll go to the wood now. It's a good thing we've got torches." Then, bidding Midge farewell, he turned to lead the others away.

His excitement rekindled, Ben followed closely. He was certain he knew what Midge had heard: the "Chop-cherry" song that the unnamed villain seemed to sing to himself. What kind of man was this? he asked himself. A murderer, according to Granny – yet an educated fellow, who had escaped the hangman and followed Dan Cutter to his home village, putting him in fear of his life – all for something with the bewildering name "The Black Onion"?

The song was running through Ben's head, and he knew that Midge Martin's ears had not been playing tricks on him at all.

He looked back over his shoulder, but already the old hawksman had vanished in the dusk.

* * *

Now the search became a good deal more serious.

In silence the watchmen followed Sam up the Tottenham path, before veering off it, deeper into the wood. The lights of the village had disappeared, and it was a comfort to everyone when the torches were lit. As the ground rose more steeply, with the trees closer together, Sam told the torch-bearers to go in front. Roger walked beside Ben with Gimlet, a long-eared hound with a rough coat, trotting at his feet.

"What did you make of Midge's tale?" Roger asked quietly. Ben realized that the young farmhand was scared – and he sensed fear among some of the other men too. Midge's words had alarmed them all.

"I'm not sure what to think," he said.

"Always knows more than he lets on, Midge does," Roger went on. "What if he's holding something back...something bad?"

"Let's keep the idle talk down, shall we, Master Graves?" Sam had overheard him, and spoke sternly. "And our eyes open!"

All at once there was a whine that startled everyone. Gimlet stopped so sharply that Roger almost tripped over him.

"What's the matter with him?" Sam asked.

The party halted. Gimlet whined again and stepped back, his tail drooping. Then he barked, making everyone jump.

"Maybe a badger or fox spooked him," one man said.

"He's not afraid of badgers or foxes," Roger retorted. "It's something else – I never saw him look so scared."

The men raised their torches high, but there was nothing to see apart from the trees. No sound was heard, save that of distant night birds.

"Try and get him to go on," Sam said to Roger. "The split tree's but a short way, if I'm not mistaken."

The young man kneeled beside Gimlet, speaking words of encouragement. Then he stood and tugged the leash, and the dog started forward again. The men followed in a close group, and soon the shape of a huge, cloven tree appeared in the torchlight.

But Gimlet stopped again – and this time he backed away, cowering fearfully against his master's legs. His expression spoke plainer than words: he would not take another step.

"Stay here with him," Sam Stubbs said. He turned to the other men, feeling for the billet at his belt. Some of them, Ben saw, were reaching for their own weapons.

"I'll take a torch, but any man who wants to wait here may do so," Sam went on. "Though I don't mind confessing, I'd prefer some company."

There was silence – then two people stepped forward. One was Isaac Cutter; the other was Ben.

"Not you!" Sam shook his head. But Ben, his curiosity at fever pitch, did not intend to miss anything.

"I'll stay close behind you," he said.

But their attention was diverted, for Isaac Cutter had seized a torch from one of the bearers. "Young Button's the bravest one here!" he snapped. "By my reckoning, this way is south towards the fallen oak. Is anyone coming?" None answered, and without looking back he strode off.

Sam took a torch from another man. "Stick close then," he muttered to Ben, "and use those keen eyes of yours!"

Ben followed him. It was only after they had gone a few yards that he realized he had forgotten to take a torch for himself. He hurried to keep near to Sam, for without a flame, the wood was in pitch darkness. Small creatures scampered away, while moths flickered in and out of the torchlight. Isaac strode restlessly ahead.

Holding his flame high, Sam quickened his pace to keep up with the old man. He and Ben hurried through the undergrowth for some distance, and Ben began wondering if Isaac had taken the wrong direction. Ahead, his torch bobbed up and down through the trees.

"This isn't right," Sam said to Ben. "If Cutter's hiding up here, his father's not the one who should search for him. How do I know he won't let him escape? So much for being sworn constable!" he muttered. "No one pays me any mind at all."

There was a shout, and quickly Sam and Ben hurried to where Isaac Cutter stood. He was looking down. In the torchlight the large trunk of a fallen tree was visible, rotten with age. But as the old man lowered his torch, Ben pointed.

"Someone's been digging under there," he said. "Just as Midge told us."

Sam crouched, and thrust his billet under the trunk. But after a moment he sat back. "There's a hole all right," he said, getting to his feet. "Big enough for a man to lie in. But as Midge said, he's long gone. Still – we'll make a sweep about just in case."

Lifting his torch, Sam moved away from the tree trunk, eyes scanning the ground. Isaac wandered off in the opposite direction. Ben realized that both men had forgotten about him, and he could go where he liked. But without light, he couldn't go far. He started to follow Sam – then froze.

It wasn't a cry, or a shout – it was a groan. And it came from no more than a few feet away!

His heart thudding, Ben stepped gingerly towards the sound. He was so intent on listening, he forgot to call for Sam… Then he heard it again. More like a moan, he thought, and he was certain of one thing now: it was human.

He peered into the dark, but could see nothing. Then he found his voice. "Over here!" he shouted. When an answering cry came, he stepped forward, only to bang his shin on a fallen branch. Wincing, he bent down, as a torch came dancing through the trees.

"Ben!" Sam cried. "Where are you?"

"Here!" Ben called, massaging his bruised leg. Soon the patch of ground about him was lit up, as Sam came crashing towards him. Cursing, the miller stumbled to a halt.

"What were you doing?" he cried. "Why didn't you stick with me?" Then he followed Ben's gaze… and let out an oath.

But Ben, the pain in his shin forgotten, took two paces forward…and at once he knew the search was over. Or at least, the search for one man was: Daniel Cutter.

But this was not the Dan Cutter Ben remembered:

a muscular fellow with thick blond hair. Despite the sound he had heard, Ben's first thought was that the man was dead.

Daniel was thin and haggard, his face bruised, his body as limp as a doll's. He was sitting on the ground, legs splayed, with his back against a tree. It looked as if his arms were hidden – until, with another shock, Ben realized they were tied behind the trunk. As Sam came forward, his torch raised, the truth was revealed – and Ben stepped back. For only now had he seen the blood. And his reaction was one of amazement, that one man could have so much of it.

It was not a trickle, it was a puddle. A vivid pool of dark red, that had soaked Dan Cutter's clothes from the waist down and stained the ground about him. Ben gazed in horror.

Another torch came up; Isaac Cutter stepped into the light and stopped, with a cry of anguish. Still Ben stared...then let out a gasp. For he had seen Dan Cutter's eyes open, and he knew he had not been mistaken when he heard the moan: the man was alive.

And as the three of them watched, his lips parted, allowing hoarse words to escape from his mouth.

"Don't let him have it," he whispered. "Don't...let him find...the Black Onion!"

Chapter Eleven

There was no question of moving Daniel Cutter, for he was dying. In fact, from the amount of blood he had lost, Sam said it was a miracle he wasn't dead already. He had been stabbed, and left bound to the tree. All they could do was untie his hands, and try to make him comfortable.

Tears ran down Isaac Cutter's cheeks as he kneeled beside his son. He called his name, but Daniel was so weak he could barely reply. He did repeat one phrase, however:

"The Black Onion... The Black Onion..."

"He's delirious," Isaac said. "Moonstruck!"

Sam crouched by the other side of the dying man. "Daniel?" he began. "It's Sam Stubbs. Can you hear me?"

There was no answer.

"I know it's hard for you to speak," Sam went on. "But I fear you've not long to live, so listen to me. I swear to you, I'll do my best to find the man who did this..." He hesitated, glancing at Isaac. "It looks to me like a sword thrust," he said quietly.

Isaac gazed at his son's blood-drenched body. "But why?" he muttered. "How has he brought this terrible fate on himself?"

There was a dullness in Daniel's eyes, but all at once he mouthed a different word: "*Scanes.*"

"Scanes?" Sam echoed. "What's that?"

And Daniel answered, so weakly that he had to force out every word. "His...name...is...Bryn...Scanes."

Ben had been told to stand back. But slowly he edged closer, straining to listen.

"Bryn Scanes?" Sam frowned. "Is he the one who robbed the justice...?" But he broke off, for Daniel's mouth was working.

"He...didn't know...where it was," he whispered. "Would have...broken into...every house in...village ...to find it." He gave a faint cough. "But...then he found me…at the old woman's."

He let out a long sigh. And the listeners leaned close, for they could see how precious each word was.

"Now he…knows it's…at Moon's," they heard. "But…couldn't…make me tell…what I didn't know myself." Daniel's mouth twitched suddenly – and to everyone's surprise, he seemed to be smiling! He gave a cough, and a bubble of blood appeared on his lips.

"Had to be…by another hand," he whispered. "The only…way…"

Isaac Cutter shook his head. "He doesn't know what he's saying," he mumbled.

But Ben was hanging on every word. Now he knew he had been right all along, when he wondered if the man who broke into the justice's house – and into Widow Luce's – was looking for something. And there was a name: Bryn Scanes. The prize this man was seeking must be so important, he would stop at nothing to get his hands on it – and the prize was the Black Onion.

Looking at Cutter's bruises, Ben realized something else: he had been tied to the tree *before* he was stabbed! Scanes had brought the unfortunate man here, and forced him to tell everything. Then when he had learned all he could, he had dealt his victim a fatal blow.

It was murder – but there was another word for what had taken place before that: torture.

"I heard you, Daniel," Sam said. "We'll go to Moon's and look for it – this Black Onion. But first, please tell me what it is!"

Isaac shook his head. "He can't hear you," he sighed. Then he stiffened, as he realized his son was trying to speak to him.

"'Twas...to be for...you, too," Daniel said, struggling to form the words. "You...and...mother..."

And now he spoke his last. "'Tis worth...a fortune," he sighed. "Beyond...a man's dreams..."

Then his eyes closed, and he was dead.

It was past midnight when Ben returned home to find his mother waiting up. Seeing how tired he was she motioned him to the table, where a rushlight burned, and brought him a warm drink. Then she sat with him while he told her what had happened.

He gave the best account he could, ending by telling her how the watchmen had wrapped Daniel Cutter's body up, made a litter of boughs and carried it to his father's house. The parson had been told, Ben said, and word sent to Justice Moon, too. Suddenly, he felt exhausted.

"You must get some rest," Mary said. "You've had a fearful time. And I'll have a few words to say to Sam, for putting you through that."

"It wasn't Sam's doing," Ben said. "I wanted to go."

"Even so," his mother countered, "that was no sight for a—" She broke off.

"A boy?" Ben managed a smile. He wanted to say that, for a boy, he had been in quite a few adventures already. And he'd seen a man stabbed before. But he thought better of it.

"Play-acting is one thing," his mother was saying. "But seeing someone really die is quite another, isn't it?"

Not wishing to talk about that now, Ben gave a nod. Instead he asked how Granny was.

"Sleeping, when I last looked. So are your brother and sister," Mary replied. Then she added: "I was going to have words with you, about this business between you and Edward. Now it must wait until tomorrow. You can come with us to Dancer's, and we'll talk there."

"But I can't," Ben said. "Sam's asked me to go with him in the morning, to the justice's house. I'm a witness to Daniel Cutter's death."

For a moment he thought his mother would utter a

sharp reply. He could hardly blame her. With one thing and another, she had seen little of him since he came home. But instead, she sighed and got up from the table.

"Very well," she said. "Come to the farm afterwards."

"I will." Ben got to his feet, but Mary's next words surprised him.

"You can't resist getting involved in some scrape or other, can you?" she mumured. "Your father was like that when he was young. Enough curiosity for two men, I always said."

Ben wanted to talk to her then about a lot of things – but feeling a yawn coming on, he asked sleepily: "Can we talk about him soon? Father, I mean?"

Mary nodded, and sent him off to bed.

When Ben and Sam arrived at Justice Moon's house the next morning, they expected to find him in a bad temper. But he listened calmly to the constable's report. Perhaps he was making an effort, since Parson Harrington was also in the room, seated by the window. It was open and the curtain pulled back, revealing the stable yard where Hal Faraway was moving about. Otherwise the laboratory looked the same: if Master Moon had tidied up, no one would have known. Meanwhile, from its cage in the corner the parrot glared at the visitors, as if to let them know they were unwelcome.

After Sam had given his account, the justice tugged his beard and said: "So, master constable, you inform me that this *Black Onion*, whatever it is, is hidden somewhere in my house. That the villain who broke in here, as well as at Widow Luce's, was seeking it, but failed to find it." Frowning, Moon drew a long breath. "And more: that having killed Daniel Cutter, this murderous fellow – Bryn Scanes by name – who even sings as he commits his heinous crimes, is likely to return here and seek it again?" He sat upright, so suddenly that both Ben and Sam blinked. "Is that what you're telling me?"

"It is, sir," Sam answered stiffly. He was sweating a little, and could not help eyeing a silver jug and cups that stood on a side chest. "It is my guess that Scanes knew the Black Onion, whatever it is, was somewhere about the village, having heard about it from Cutter when they were both in prison – so when they were freed, he followed him here. It seems at first he didn't know where Cutter was, to force the exact hiding place out of him. That's why he started breaking into places, anywhere he thought the Onion might be, see?" Sam drew a deep breath. "He started with the biggest house in Hornsey – yours. And now I've learned that the house burgled in Crux End was the biggest there too, though the owners were away and luckily their valuables were locked up. If Scanes hadn't found Cutter, he would have gone on breaking into other houses. And then...well, you've heard the rest."

Having said his piece, Sam waited. Moon looked at Parson Harrington, who had arrived just before Ben and Sam, but had said little so far. Now he spoke up.

"What a terrible business," he murmured, with a shake of his head, "And the nub of the matter is that this wicked Scanes fellow, having killed one man already, seems likely to come back here, as the constable says, and try again."

At that, the justice's composure finally broke. Getting to his feet, he thumped the desk. "Perhaps now you'll heed me, master constable, when I ask you again to place a watch on my house!" he cried. "I mean armed men, day and night. Or do you want us all to be murdered in our beds?"

"No, sir, I don't intend to let that happen," Sam answered, trying his best to sound firm. "I'll keep watch myself, and gather some other fellows—"

"Do so!" Moon snapped. "And take care to pick men who will stay awake and alert!"

He turned to the parson. "By the heavens," he exclaimed, "can all this fuss truly be about an onion? And why black – with mould? A poor man's food, sold by the string for a couple of pennies in any market? Can we not guess what this mysterious prize could be, that drives men to such lengths as murder?" He raised his hands helplessly, and sat down again. "What on earth," he finished lamely, "can a *Black Onion* be?"

Through the open window, skylarks could be heard. A bluebottle buzzed in, circled round and flew out again. But as Ben pondered the mystery to himself once again, the parson stood up and took a couple of paces round the room. He had clearly been puzzling over the matter too.

"What if you were mistaken?" he asked thoughtfully, looking in turn at Sam and Ben. "What if it wasn't 'Onion' you heard? Suppose it was 'Union'?"

Justice Moon stared. "Black Union?" he said. "That makes no sense either. Unless…" Then he gave a start. "Unless you mean the Latin word?"

The two men looked at each other, whereupon Master Moon smacked the desk again, so violently that several books crashed to the floor. At once, the parrot set up a fearful screeching.

"Dolt! See what you've done! See what you've done!"

"Silence!" Seizing a scrap of paper, Master Moon

screwed it into a ball and flung it at the bird, who lapsed into angry squawks. Then, excitedly, he faced the parson again.

"Of course – Latin *union*! What a joy it is, to have another university man here!" he cried. "Harrington, you're a marvel!"

The parson, who disliked the justice's outbursts, gave a nod. Seeing the puzzled look on Sam's face, he explained. "A union is a large pearl," he said. "Jewellers use the word. So a 'black union' could mean a black pearl – a rare and precious gem. And one that may indeed drive some men to murder!"

Sam stifled an oath, but Ben felt a stab of excitement. He wished he understood Latin, as learned men did, for he felt sure that if he had known what "Union" meant, he too could have worked out the answer. Now, it all made sense! Granny, who was rather deaf, had simply repeated the word she thought she had heard: onion. But since everyone knew an onion was almost worthless – let alone a blackened one – it had been a mystery. And as for Dan Cutter: it had been hard to make out anything he said. If only he had lived long enough to tell more ...

Another thought struck Ben, one that saddened him. He turned to Sam, and realized the same thought had occurred to him too.

"That's why Dan Cutter said it was worth a fortune," Sam said grimly. "And that's what he meant when he said it was for his mother and father too. Cutter may have stolen a precious pearl, but in his rough way, he was going to try and use it to redeem himself. He meant to give money to his parents – maybe even to mend his ways, as they'd always hoped. Yet he left it too late!"

"And paid the highest price of all," Parson Harrington added. Turning gravely to Moon, he said: "Now if you will excuse me, master justice, I will visit Isaac and his wife to see what comfort I might offer."

Moon looked shaken. "While I," he muttered, "will have to turn my house upside down, until this great pearl is found – assuming we can take Cutter's word that it is really here. I still find that hard to believe – for I know I've never set eyes on it! You're certain the man didn't give any hint as to where it might be, exactly?"

Sam shook his head. "He said he couldn't tell what he didn't know himself," he answered. "But he wasn't making much sense, by then."

With a sigh, Moon got up to see the parson out. As he left, Harrington turned to Sam.

"I'll make enquiries about this Black Union," he

said. "I know a jeweller in Goldsmith's Row in London, who may be able to help. In the meantime, master constable, we must look to you to make what plans you think best."

The two men went out, and Sam turned to Ben. "I'll have to get someone to run the mill for me," he said. "For now I've really got my hands full!"

"I can help, if I'm still your unofficial under-constable, that is," Ben said.

"Well, I'm going to need all the help I can get," Sam replied seriously. "And one thing you can do is ask Dancer if he'll be one of the watchmen on the justice's house."

Ben agreed. From the hallway, the two of them heard Justice Moon bid farewell to the parson. Then a sound made Ben look round sharply, towards the open window.

Hal Faraway was outside, peeping round the edge of the window frame. The moment Ben caught his eye, the boy jumped like a rabbit and vanished. But Ben knew right away that Hal had been listening the whole time.

And from the frightened look on his face, he must have heard every word that had been said.

Chapter Twelve

*N*ow there was real fear in the village. Daniel Cutter's terrible death, let alone the news that a murderer was stalking the countryside, had fallen like a thunderbolt upon the people of Hornsey. For safety, they banded together. Those who lived alone or in isolated cottages made plans to stay with friends, while old people were taken in by their relatives. Sam quickly made it known that the only place Bryn Scanes was likely to strike now was at the justice's, which would be guarded day and night. But people were not reassured – and among the most discontented was Dancer May.

"So Stubbs wants my help, does he?" he demanded, when Ben brought Sam's request later that morning. "Well, that's no surprise. I've said all along he wasn't up to the task!"

Ben was standing in Dancer's kitchen with his mother. Edward and Margery were outside, and Ellen had gone to market. Ben had told Mary and Dancer what had occurred at Moon's. He went on to say that Sam had asked him to help search the justice's house. The more people the better, Sam had said.

"Why, the cheek of the man!" Dancer cried. "He asks boys to do his work for him. What next? Will he want Margery too?"

"He needs as many pairs of eyes as he can get," Ben replied. "And I'd like to help him."

"Raising the hue and cry is the constable's business," Dancer told him. "Especially when there's a murderer on the loose." He swallowed. "It needs stout men, not boys," he went on. "Men who can carry arms, and…" He broke off, and gave a cough. Moving to the table where a pitcher of water stood, he splashed some into a mug and took a gulp.

"Your pardon…something stuck in my throat," he explained to Mary. "Are you thirsty?" he muttered, glancing at Ben. "Help yourself to a drink."

"I'm all right," Ben said. Once again he thought Dancer looked uneasy. And seeing the expression on his mother's face, he saw that she was thinking the same.

"I think Ben should go back and help Sam," she said. "He's always been good at finding things that were lost. As for being stout..." She met Dancer's eye. "He showed courage in the wood last night, didn't he? As much as most grown men would."

Dancer blinked. Then without another word, he turned on his heel and went out.

Taken aback, Ben waited for his mother to speak. But when she did, her words were not what he expected.

"Before you go off, I want you to make your peace with Edward," she said. "Do you promise me you'll do that?"

Ben nodded, and seeing that she had no more to say, took his leave. His mind was busy – and not just with what he now knew as the Black Union. Because one thing cheered him above all else: whatever Dancer thought, Ben knew that his mother was proud of him.

He found Edward in the barn, breaking open a bale of straw. Seeing Ben walk in, his brother made a big show of spreading the straw in a corner.

"I've got to make a bed up," he said. "There's a cow sick – Margery's bringing her in. It's garget, Dancer says. That's a swelling in its throat and tongue."

"I remember," Ben said. He hoped Edward was not going to start calling him a town boy again. "You have to wash the cow's mouth out with vinegar, don't you?"

"Dancer will know what to do." Edward shrugged. But when he turned round, there was a worried look on his face. "You know what they say?" he muttered. "Garget's caused by a bad spirit that flies through the air. That's what's come to Hornsey, isn't it? Something evil. We never had a robbery before – let alone a murder."

"You've heard what's happened, then?" Ben said.

"Who hasn't?" Edward replied, frowning. "I still don't think it fair that you were one of the night watchmen and not me," he went on. "But I can't say I envy you, finding Dan Cutter bleeding to death like that."

Ben seized the moment. "I'm sorry we got off on the wrong foot that first day."

Edward looked embarrassed "Well, you're here now," he said. "Dancer wanted me to show you round..." Then, seeing Ben's expression, he glared. "Don't tell me – you're too busy!"

"I've got to help Sam," Ben said. Despite everything, Edward made him feel ashamed again. "Mother's agreed," he added – too late.

"Go, then!" Edward cried. "Go off with Sam, and the justice. That's what you're used to in London, isn't it? Mixing with important people..." Seizing a handful of straw, he threw it down angrily. "Leave us peasants to get on with our labours!"

With that, he turned his back. Soon he was stamping the straw down with his foot, much flatter than it needed to be.

Ben left him and went outside. But within an hour, Edward's words had been driven from his mind. For after a bite of dinner at the justice's, he found himself caught up in the search for the Black Union.

It was a tense business. Sam, Doll Fisher and Hal Faraway were scouring the big house from top to bottom, while Justice Moon hovered about, grumbling. Roger Graves had come from the village to help too. He insisted on bringing Gimlet, though no one could see how the dog would help him find a black pearl, no matter how big. Sam decided it was best that Roger search the stables and outbuildings, with Hal helping him.

As far as Doll Fisher was concerned, it was all a fool's exercise. She and Ben searched the kitchen, even though Doll knew every inch of the room, and swore that if anything had been concealed she would have seen it. "But does His Emptiness listen to me?" she demanded, standing on tiptoe to look along a shelf. "Of course not. We're dolts, all of us!"

Ben was near the fireplace, peering at the brickwork. Thinking of Widow Luce's chimney, he decided he would check to see if there was a gap anywhere. But though the mortar was cracked in places, there was no cavity.

"You know what he had the nerve to say once, young Ben?" Doll went on. "He said he has better conversations with that parrot than with me! You see what insults I've to bear?"

Ben straightened up. He liked Mistress Doll, despite her sharp tongue. "You were right – there's nothing hidden here," he said. "Where do we go next?"

"Upstairs, I suppose," Doll muttered. "Though I bet my best petticoat we'll find nothing there either." She sighed. "There's no pearl, Ben. Why would Dan Cutter hide it here? And in any case, how could he have got in without leaving any sign? None of it makes sense to me."

But Ben did not share Doll's opinion. He had watched Daniel Cutter die, and heard his testimony. No man would tell a lie so readily with his dying breath. And more, Ben could not forget his hoarse, whispered words: *...couldn't make me tell what I didn't know myself...*

On his walk down from the Hog's Back, Ben had been thinking about that. He also remembered Cutter saying: *It had to be by another hand...the only way...*

Unlike Sam, Ben was not so inclined to think Cutter had been delirious when he'd said that. If the man did not know exactly where the pearl was, he reasoned, then somebody else must be involved – an accomplice. It seemed the only explanation: someone Cutter knew, and had perhaps paid to conceal the precious jewel? Another idea struck Ben: perhaps the accomplice did not even know what it was he had hidden?

He mulled this idea over. The jewel could be wrapped or enclosed in something. If only he had some idea what it looked like. He did not know how big a pearl could be...as large as a hazelnut perhaps, or even a walnut? Might it even be as big as an egg?

"Sixpence for your thoughts! For, by the look on your face, they must be worth more than a mere penny!"

Jolted out of his daydream, Ben looked round at Doll. "Come on," she went on. "I'll tell His Emptiness we found nothing in the kitchen. Wait until you see the look on *his* face!"

The two of them climbed the creaking staircase to the landing of the old house. There they found Sam on his knees, poking about in a big oak chest. At once Doll called out, making him start.

"There's naught in there but clean linen!" she cried. "So don't you go dirtying it!" She walked up and slammed the lid of the chest, just missing Sam's fingers. "If anyone's really hidden this jewel somewhere, it wouldn't be in so obvious a place as that, would it?" she snapped. "If you ask me, 'tis all a fable anyway!"

As Sam got to his feet there was a creak, and a familiar face appeared on the stairs. "What's this, a gathering of gossips?" the justice demanded. "Pray continue your search! And I don't wish to hear your voice again," he said to Doll, "until you tell me you've searched every nook and cranny!"

"Old goat," Doll muttered. She waited until her master had gone, and the door to the laboratory banged shut. "We've looked high and low," she told Sam. "There's nothing hidden."

"I've been up to the attic, under the roof," Sam

said. "It's full of old junk, thick with dust."

"I could have told you that," Doll retorted. "Apart from the bedchambers, we don't use the top floors." She glanced towards a closed door. "Save for that room," she said. "The one His Emptiness keeps locked."

Ben's eyes widened: the locked chamber! He remembered how angry Justice Moon had become when Sam had asked him about it. Intrigued, he gazed at the heavy door. Seeing that it led to a room at the front of the house, he remembered the moment when he had stood outside, on his first day in Hornsey. He had looked up at a window, and seen a flash of light...

"Do you know what's in there?" he asked.

"Something to do with his experiments." Doll gave a snort. "I ask you, is that any way for a man to spend his time? Puzzling over books and charts, and gazing at the stars?"

"Well, the lock looks stout enough," Sam observed. "I take it the justice has a key?"

"The only key," Doll answered.

Suddenly Ben remembered something Margery had told him. "I've heard Justice Moon has a stone that floats," he said. "Is that what he keeps in there?"

"Nay, young Ben, that's a lodestone," Doll told

him. "It's in the laboratory – and it doesn't float. It sits on a little board, in a dish of water." She sighed. "You don't want to pay any mind to those tales that go about the village. His Emptiness is no alchemist, or conjuring man...else he'd have turned me into a cockroach long ago!"

In spite of herself, she broke into a laugh. Ben smiled, and glanced at Sam. But the constable was glum faced.

"You know what this means?" he said. "Since we've looked in every room, we'll have to take up the floorboards."

Doll's smile faded. "Well, I can guess what His Emptiness would say to that," she said dryly. "But you're constable, so I'll let you tell him."

It was evening when Sam finally called a halt to the fruitless task. Floorboards had been lifted and put down again. Cupboards, chests and closets had been peered into and cobwebs disturbed, but there was no black pearl anywhere. Now everyone was tired, especially the justice. He had searched the laboratory again, by himself, not wanting anyone else present. As for the locked chamber, to Sam's relief there was no argument. Justice Moon had looked in it that morning, he said, and there was nothing hidden there either. So that was the end of the matter.

Ben and Sam came to the laboratory to take their leave. The parrot clucked in its corner.

"*Go away! Leave me alone!*"

Irritably its master turned to the fruit bowl, picked out a pear and bit off its tip. "Here – stop your mouth with this," he muttered. He went to the cage and poked the morsel through the bars.

"*When as the rye reach to the chin,*" the parrot squawked. "*And chop-cherry, chop-cherry ripe within...*"

"Enough!" Moon tapped the bars. The parrot hopped to the floor of the cage and started eating.

But Ben's pulse had quickened. Again, the "Chop-cherry" song... He glanced round. His eyes were drawn to the justice's globe, his books and scrolls. Now he saw the lodestone, in a corner: a dull-looking lump of rock, resting in a bowl of water as Doll had told him. Bryn Scanes had searched this very room, Ben thought. Yet the man had been unable to find the Black Union, just as they had... Where on earth could it be?

Then Ben gave a start. "Scanes...he left Dan Cutter for dead, didn't he?" he exclaimed.

Sam looked puzzled. "You know he did..."

"So he doesn't know we heard his last words," Ben went on. "He won't realize we're expecting him."

"All the better," Sam said, understanding Ben's meaning now. "If he turns up, we can nab him!"

"I hope so," Justice Moon snapped. "As I hope you've chosen men who are fit for the task!"

"I'll take one watch myself, sir," Sam replied, though he sounded tired enough to sleep where he stood. "Master Graves will stay, too. He'll have his dog with him."

The justice nodded curtly. And since all seemed to have been said, Sam and Ben made their way out.

The sun was going down, and birds were gathering to roost in nearby trees. Roger appeared round the corner of the house, leading Gimlet.

"I was coming to look for you," he said. "There's something odd about that boy, Hal."

"Odd?" Sam stifled a yawn. "How so?"

"He was jumping about like a scared puppy all the time I searched the stable," Roger answered. "I thought he was scared of Scanes coming back – can't blame him for that, can you? I told him there would be watchmen, but he didn't seem to like that either. He made Gimlet nervous, too."

"I meant to question him anyway," Sam said. "I'll

have a word with him now, then snatch a couple of hours' sleep. Will you keep watch until then?" When Roger gave a nod, he turned to Ben. "You'd better get home before dark," he said. "Your mother will worry…"

"Can I come along while you speak to Hal?" Ben asked.

Sam frowned. "What for?"

Ben was hiding his excitement. For no sooner had he heard Roger's words than a sudden suspicion had formed in his mind: the accomplice!

Someone who could have got into the house, who might know places to hide the Black Union… He saw again the crafty look on Hal Faraway's face the day they met. A horse-courser's boy…a skipjack…could he really be trusted?

"Well, I'm interested," Ben began, but Sam was shaking his head.

"It's late. If I need you, I'll send word—"

He broke off, and turned round sharply. Roger turned too, as did Ben, for they all heard it: a thud of hooves from the stable yard. Gimlet barked and leaped up, tugging at his leash – and in an instant, they understood.

"He's got the justice's horse!" Sam cried.

He took off with Ben at his heels – and as soon as

they rounded the back of the house, they saw they were not mistaken.

Some yards away, Hal Faraway was perched astride Justice Moon's horse, kicking at its sides with his bare feet. As Ben and Sam ran into view he looked round, then jerked the reins – the horse, Ben saw, was saddled and bridled. Already it was moving off, along the path that led around the house. But it was an old nag, slow to gain speed – and Hal had not reckoned on being chased. He urged the animal round the corner, with Ben in pursuit. Behind, Gimlet was barking excitedly.

Hal rode his mount towards the paddock gate, which was open. In a moment horse and rider were through it – but all Ben did was run faster.

And to his triumph, he was gaining on his quarry!

Chapter Thirteen

*I*n the twilight, Ben raced across the paddock. The horse was only a short way ahead of him but it was gaining speed, from a trot to a canter. If Hal brought it to a gallop, Ben would never catch up with him. The boy was an experienced rider, lying flat along the horse's neck, his shirt loose behind him. Having no stirrups, he was guiding the animal with his legs. There was a fence ahead and, suddenly, Ben saw that Hal meant to force his mount to jump over it.

"Stop – it's too high!" he shouted, but to no avail:

Hal was about to take the risk. He spoke into the horse's ear, then gave a shout and clapped his heels against its flanks. All Ben could do was watch as the animal whinnied and lurched forward – then, only a few feet from the obstacle, it stopped dead. In dismay Ben saw the horse fold its front legs and drop to its knees, sending Hal flying from the saddle and sailing over the fence, to land in a heap on the other side.

There was a moment in which Ben was aware of shouting behind him, and Gimlet barking. Then he darted forward, peering through the bars at the spot where Hal had fallen...only to see the boy get up, shake himself like a dog and run off.

At once Ben was after him. Avoiding the horse, which was on its feet now and looking none the worse for its adventure, he clambered over the paddock fence and dropped down. Then he was sprinting through open meadow, thinking fast. If Hal crossed the Newington road, he could disappear in Tottenham Wood, and Ben would never find him.

His breath came in bursts. Ahead, he saw Hal drawing away from him. The boy was faster on his feet than Ben, and less tired. Ben tried to put on a final spurt, but it was not enough. Soon, he thought, his body would give up – whereupon Hal made one mistake.

Still running at speed through the long grass, he turned to look behind – and stumbled, falling onto all fours. Though he was quickly on his feet again, those seconds made all the difference. But when Ben caught up with him, he met with something he had not expected: Hal simply dropped to one knee and, using Ben's own momentum, seized him by the arm and flung him over his shoulder.

It was Ben's turn to land heavily in the grass. Panting, he got up, remembering too late Hal's words that day they had first encountered each other: *I've won prizes at wrestling matches...*

It was no bluff. Ben had been outmatched before, but usually by older boys than this. Now he found himself jerked to his feet, his arm thrust behind him – and a set of bony fingers clamped around his windpipe.

"You've two choices, Button," Hal hissed in his ear. "Let me get away – or I throttle you!"

Blood rushed to Ben's head. With his free hand he grabbed Hal's wrist, but all the boy did was squeeze harder.

"Let me away, or else!"

Ben was wheezing: at this rate he would pass out, for he hadn't the strength to wrench Hal's hand from his throat. He tried to free his other arm, but Hal merely pushed it further up his back. He tried to stamp on Hal's foot, but the other flicked it aside. Whichever move he made, this boy was ready for him.

Again he heard shouts, but they seemed far away. And with the light growing faint, he feared that Sam and Roger would not see him. Breathlessly he spoke up. "They'll track you with the dog," he began – but his voice was choked off.

"Two choices!" Hal repeated. "Make one, quick!"

Though he was growing dizzy, somehow Ben's mind still worked. Not much of a choice, he thought vaguely, as shapes danced before his eyes. The shapes became faces – and one of them looked like his friend, Matt Fields. Then all at once Ben knew what to do – what Matt would have done: he gave a gurgle and went limp. His eyes closed, and he sagged like a dead weight in Hal's arms.

To Ben's relief, Hal stepped back, cursed, and let his captive fall to the ground. But as he turned to run off, Ben's hand shot out to grab his bare foot. Hal toppled over but squirmed round, seizing his opponent's leg. In a moment he would use some other wrestling hold and gain the advantage, but Ben was not about to let that happen.

Releasing Hal's foot, he quickly drew his dagger.

Then he sank to his knees, and pressed its point to Hal's neck.

"Now *you've* a choice," he gasped. "Talk, or I spit you!"

Hal relaxed, letting go of Ben's leg. He lay on his side, panting.

"You heard," Ben went on – but his reply was a harsh laugh.

"Don't try your tricks with me again, player boy!" Hal said. "You're no dagger-man!"

"But I've got a voice that can fill a theatre," Ben said. "If I shout loud enough..."

It worked. "So, what do you want?" Hal demanded. "I haven't wronged you, have I?"

"You've wronged a lot of people," Ben said. He was getting his breath back now. "Your master, for one. It was you who hid the Black Union for Dan Cutter, wasn't it?"

"I don't know what you're talking about!" came the retort.

Someone called from the paddock. All Ben had to do was shout back – and he knew Hal would guess that too.

"I think Cutter told you to hide the pearl," Ben persisted. "Somewhere only you could find it. Then, even if he were caught, he couldn't tell where it was.

But it cost him his life! You didn't expect that, did you?"

Hal drew a sharp breath. "Wait," he said – and for the first time he looked afraid.

"Listen," he went on. "I'll tell you, if you'll let me go. If you don't, my life's not worth a farthing anyway. What can the justice do – or Stubbs, come to that – but give me a flogging? You think I haven't been through worse?"

But Ben was in no mood to bargain. In his mind's eye he saw Dan Cutter, gasping his last words. He saw Isaac, kneeling forlornly beside his son's body...

"It won't only be a flogging," Ben said. "You'll go to prison – to Newgate, or maybe the Clink. Have you seen them? I have. You'll be burned through the ear – then likely they'll hang you anyway..."

Hal's hand came up to seize his wrist, but Ben merely pressed the dagger harder to his skin. "Talk," he snapped, sounding as if he meant it. "You're running out of time!"

All at once Hal gave in. "Listen then, Button," he breathed, "and when I've finished, you tell me if you'd have done things any different!"

And in a shaky voice, he told his story.

"A week ago, Cutter came by. I was exercising the horse, and I met him on the road. He'd been walking fast, all the way from London, and he was scared." Hal paused. "He saw me for what I was...and he knew I wouldn't refuse a gold half sovereign. More money than I've ever had in my life!"

"So he paid you to hide the black pearl," Ben said, managing to hide his excitement. At last, he was getting to the heart of the mystery. "What does it look like?"

Hal gave a snort. "What do you think a black pearl looks like?"

Ben hesitated – then another thought struck him. "Were you not tempted to steal it yourself?" he asked.

"He didn't look like a man to tangle with," Hal muttered. "Anyway, he promised me another half sovereign. He was going to find somewhere to hide, then come back for the pearl when it was safe – soon, he said. I didn't know things would turn out so badly, did I?"

Suddenly the boy sounded desperate. "I heard you and Stubbs talking to the justice," he said. "That's how I know Scanes will have found out the Black Union's here – he'll know it was me Cutter paid to conceal it!

"Don't you see, Button?" he cried. "He'll come for me! And yes, I would have taken it – today, if there hadn't been people all over the house! Now it's too late…and you talk of prison?" He almost spat the word. "I'd rather face prison than fall into Scanes's hands," he went on. "You should have seen Cutter's face when he told me of that fellow…you don't know what you're up against, player boy!"

Ben stared at Hal. Having seen Cutter die, he understood why the boy had said his life would not be worth a farthing. For a second his attention wandered from the dagger – and it was all the time Hal needed.

There was a thud, and Ben's head rocked backwards. Hal's knee had come up, cracking him in the face. He slumped to the ground, and everything went dark.

At first it sounded like a hum of insects, until Ben realized he could hear voices. He was lying on something soft, though he could see nothing at all. The voices grew louder…then he recognized one of them.

"Only bruising," Rattling Sam was saying. "He needs rest…"

"He certainly does! And what were you thinking of, letting him go charging off like that?"

It was his mother. Ben opened his eyes, but around him all was still dark. He grew uneasy – had he been blinded? He was about to speak when the cloth was snatched from his face, and at once he could see. Relief swept over him.

"You're awake." His mother's face was close to his. "You were knocked out," she went on. "Sam and Roger found you...you've been senseless for a while. Are you hurting?"

Ben's surroundings came into focus. He was in a large bed with hangings of red velvet – grander than any he had ever seen, let alone been in. His gaze wandered about the candlelit room. He saw the gleam of silver plate, and portraits on the walls.

"Where am I?" he asked.

"In the justice's bedchamber," Mary told him. "He insisted. He says you were very brave to give chase as you did."

Ben drew a breath, as the events came back to him. "Hal! Where is he...?"

"We lost him – he ran like the wind. No one will see him again, I reckon." Sam was standing by the bed. Beyond his shoulder Ben saw Roger, looking anxious.

"Gimlet gave chase," Roger said. "But he came back, tail between his legs." The young man sighed. "If truth be told, he never was much of a tracker."

Ben was eager to tell what he had found out.

"Scanes will know that it was Hal who hid the Black Union for Cutter," he said. "That's why Hal took off like he did—"

"Enough – stop!" Ben's mother gripped his hand. "Tell it to the justice tomorrow," she said. "The hour's late, and you need to recover. Doll will make you a posset – hot milk curdled with wine. It'll help you sleep."

Ben sighed, but he knew his mother was right. Besides, his head was aching. "Am I badly bruised?" he asked. "John will scold me when he sees me. He'll make me wear thick smelly paste to hide it when I go onstage again…"

At that, Sam laughed loudly and, as the others joined in, Ben realized they were laughing with relief that he was his old self again.

"Sorry," Ben muttered. "I know there are more important things to think about…"

"Maybe – but heed your mother." Sam leaned forward and squeezed Ben's shoulder. "Your bruise will heal, and your words will wait till morning. Meanwhile, I'd make the most of the justice's hospitality. I don't suppose you sleep in a bed like this very often!"

With a smile Ben closed his eyes, and soon drifted off to sleep. He awoke a short while later, with Doll

Fisher at his bedside, and sat up to take the warm, spicy drink she gave him. Then he lay back, and slept on until late morning.

Justice Moon sat at his desk, wearing a grim expression. He looked tired, perhaps from having to sleep in one of his dusty spare bedchambers. But he was civil to Ben, praising him for his pursuit of Hal Faraway.

"To think I trusted that boy!" he exclaimed, shaking his head. "I brought him here, gave him work and a home... I've said it before: I can't keep servants!"

Ben's forehead still throbbed where it had been struck by Hal's knee, but he felt a lot better. It was almost midday, and he was embarrassed to have slept so late in Justice Moon's huge bed. But after a bowl of Doll's porridge, he had been keen to get dressed and come downstairs. He was allowed to sit on a stool while he told his story.

Sam, who had to stand, was looking unhappy. He had endured a tongue-lashing from the justice for letting Hal escape. But the worst thing was that, despite Ben's quick thinking, the boy had got away without saying where he had hidden the Black Union.

So in one way they were none the wiser. The justice was still grumbling about having to search the house all over again, when Parson Harrington arrived. And it was then that everything changed.

First of all the parson wanted to hear a full account of the previous day's events for himself – and, by the end of it, he looked quite excited. It turned out that he had stayed in London overnight, and had only just returned. Now he told what he had learned from the jeweller in Goldsmith's Row.

"The Black Union," he began. "If I'd known precisely what it was, let alone where it came from, I confess I would have been even more alarmed. In fact, master justice –" he met Moon's eye – "I would have sent word to the Queen – for by rights this prize belongs to her!"

And when Ben and Sam exchanged startled looks, Harrington told his tale. It began not in Newgate Prison, as Granny Jenkin's account had done, nor anywhere else in England...but on the Atlantic Ocean.

"Let me draw you a picture," the parson said, "of a huge carrack in full sail on the high seas – a galleon, named the *San Felipe*. As you will guess, the name is Spanish, for this was no less a vessel than one of King Philip of Spain's treasure ships. The kind that cross the world, carrying riches from the Spanish Indies. Sometimes our seamen manage to seize one and bring it back to England, but such an event is rare. And, most rare, was the capture of a certain ship laden with silk and spices, gold, silver and jewels – the whole cargo, it's said, amounting to more than one hundred thousand English pounds!"

Ben blinked, while Sam Stubbs's jaw dropped. But Moon startled everyone by giving one of his thumps on the desk. "The *San Felipe* – I remember it!" he cried. "That was in the spring of 1587 – Sir Francis Drake himself captured it off the Azores! One of his greatest prizes, which he brought into Plymouth. Why, the Queen's share alone would fill a dozen coffers!"

The justice took a breath. "So, Harrington – are you telling us that our black pearl came from the *San Felipe*'s hoard? Is this the jewel that has caused one man's death, and put the people of a whole village in fear of their lives?"

"It is indeed." The parson nodded. "And do you also remember what befell the *San Felipe,* while it lay in Plymouth harbour?"

"I do," Moon answered. "The ship was shamefully looted, and a good deal of her treasure lost!"

"So the cargo was treasure trove," Ben broke in.

"Isn't that what they call it, when it's meant for the crown?"

"They do, Master Button," the parson answered. "And the Black Union was stolen from that trove – by a sailor perhaps, while the ship lay at anchor. Sentries were bribed, and some seamen filled their pockets and deserted. An outrage, I would call it." He sighed, shaking his head.

"But at least the mystery is made plain," the justice said. "This great pearl changed hands, from one thief to another – and ended up in the possession of Daniel Cutter. No wonder he thought its price was beyond his dreams. And no wonder this villain Scanes spared no pains to pursue him and get his hands on it!"

He broke off, looking at Harrington. "You've discovered much from your jeweller," he said. "Did he also tell you how big the fabled Black Union is, so that we may picture what we've been looking for? Then perhaps, we might guess at last where it is hidden!"

Everyone waited for the answer, whereupon an unwelcome sound made them all start.

"When as the rye reach to the chin,
And chop-cherry, chop-cherry ripe within…"

"Silence, you wretched bird!" Moon stood up,

looking for something to throw...then he blinked as Ben suddenly jumped to his feet.

The men turned as, with his heart quickening, Ben pointed across the room towards the table with the globe – and the dish of fruit.

"It...it wouldn't happen to be the size of a cherry, would it?" he asked. "A black cherry?"

Chapter Fourteen

The three men stared at Ben in silence. Slowly they turned their eyes to the fruit bowl, which was piled with pears, plums, an apple or two...and cherries.

"*Wretched bird!*" the parrot squawked. "*Chop-cherry ripe...*"

It ceased when Justice Moon moved towards the table. But if it expected to receive a tasty treat, it was going to be disappointed. Instead the justice peered down at the fruit, as if afraid of what he might find.

"Master Button..." He turned to Ben, his face even

paler than usual. "Would you come over here?"

Ben went to the table. So did Sam and the parson. The same question was on everyone's lips: could the Black Union really have been under their noses the whole time?

Then suddenly, they all started talking at once.

"Is it possible?" Harrington exclaimed.

"What made you think of it?" Sam asked.

"Within my sight, every single day?" the justice cried. "It cannot be!"

"It's...it's just a theory," Ben said. "I could be wrong."

"Then let's find out, shall we?"

It was Harrington who spoke last. Watched by the others, he began picking the pears, plums and apples out of the bowl and placing them on the tabletop. When only black cherries remained, he took the first one up and squeezed it.

Juicy, dark pulp appeared on the parson's fingers. Dropping the cherry, he picked up another, which he also squashed. A third received the same treatment, but still at least a score of them remained.

Ben's pulse was racing. Had he stumbled on the answer? Despite his sore head, he had been thinking hard about the Black Union. If he were Hal, he had wondered, where would he hide such a thing? Was there a place no one would look? Then a notion had come to him in a flash: where better than in full view, among objects that so closely resembled it?

And now he saw it! One cherry, slightly darker than its fellows – and too round. It had no dimple, but was a perfect sphere, like the globe that stood close by. For of course, it wasn't a cherry...

Ben pointed and the parson stiffened. Wiping his juice-stained fingers on his sleeve, he took up the black sphere and frowned.

He squeezed it, but it did not yield. He squeezed it again, harder – then held it up and stared at it. Finally he turned to Ben.

"My brightest pupil!" he cried. "Have I not always said so?"

Sam and the justice were dumbfounded. Neither could take his eyes off the huge pearl, for now there was no mistake. It had a lustre unlike any fruit. It was smooth as a sea-washed pebble, and as big as a grape...

It was the Black Union.

Moon held out his hand, and gently the parson laid the pearl on his palm. After gazing at it, then holding it to the light, the justice turned to the others with a look of wonder.

"Remarkable," he murmured. "To think of the

years this has taken to grow, lying on some distant seabed...to be plucked from its shell, then shipped to Spain, only to be captured by Sir Francis Drake himself! And to end up, by so many winding ways, here in my laboratory. Truly remarkable!"

He looked at Ben. "You've earned the right to hold this," he said. "For it was you who solved the puzzle!"

Ben took the Black Union from Moon's hand and stared at it. Thoughts flew about in his head. The search was over, but he knew the story wasn't – not yet.

"It was your parrot that solved it, sir," he said. "The 'Chop-cherry' song made me think of – well, of cherries."

Sam found his voice at last. "Well, Ben, you've the sharpest wits of anyone I know," he said. "And you've done my job for me too!" Then a thought struck him. "Might there be some reward for such a valuable thing, sir?" he asked Moon. "I mean, when it's given to the Queen?"

"Perhaps," the justice answered. "Especially when Her Majesty hears the whole tale. But if there is," he added, "there are many who deserve a share, don't you think?"

His question was directed to the parson. "It would be a fitting end to this dreadful business," Harrington agreed. "If the Queen pleases, a reward could be shared among the poorest in the village – like Isaac and Agnes Cutter. And those who have been wronged, like Widow Luce – your grandmother too, Master Button."

He smiled at Ben, who felt very relieved. It might be a way to bring some good from the matter, if that was possible. Now even the justice was smiling. Sam slapped Ben on the back and said he was a stout fellow...then his face clouded.

"You look troubled, master constable," Harrington said.

"I am," Sam answered thoughtfully. "We may have found the prize – but there's a man out there somewhere who still thinks it's hidden in this house. A man who'll risk anything to get it. Indeed, I'm thankful he didn't come last night. But I'll bet all I have that this same man won't waste any more time coming back here – I feel it in my bones!"

Another silence fell – and, to Ben, it seemed as if a cold hand had touched his heart. He mouthed the words to himself: *Bryn Scanes*.

The afternoon was waning as Ben strolled up to the Hog's Back. He walked slowly, not because he was tired or hurting, for his headache had ceased. He was thinking over what he would say – how he would explain to his mother that he was going to be part of a trap. A trap that was being set to catch a murderer.

Ben had forgotten whose plan it was. Once the word *trap* had been uttered, the idea had grown quickly. And after the justice, the parson and the constable had turned it about, they agreed their course of action. Scanes would lose no more time, they reasoned – it was likely he would strike that night. Before dark, armed men must be posted around the house. There would be lookouts hidden by the road too so that from whatever direction the man came, he would be spotted. Meanwhile, the justice said, the Black Union would be placed under lock and key, and he himself would guard it, armed with a pistol. There was one difficulty, however – and that part of the plan was Ben's.

"It seems likely Scanes knows it was the stable boy who hid the Black Union," the justice had said. "So I feel certain he will seek him out first – but now Hal is gone."

Silence had followed – until Ben spoke up. "Do you think he knows what Hal looks like?" he had asked. Whereupon the justice had replied that he doubted it, since Scanes had only been to the house at night, and he hadn't entered the stable...but then Sam had interrupted him.

"Your pardon, sir, but I see where this is leading. Surely you're not willing for Ben to put his life in danger, by play-acting the stable boy? This man we're after is a murderer!"

The justice had looked uncomfortable. So had the parson – until Ben had seized his chance.

"But a player is what I am. A stable boy's an easy enough role...and who else will take it?"

Now, as Ben drew near to Dancer's farm, he wondered how his mother would take the news. She would be afraid for him, of course – she might forbid his taking part. At the least, she would be angry with Sam for involving Ben in such a dangerous scheme. As for the justice and the parson, Ben thought, even those two important men would find it hard to stand up to Mistress Button when the safety of her children was at stake. In fact, the more Ben thought about it, the more foolhardy his plan might look. Although no harm should come to him – for Sam had sworn he would be nearby, well-armed – he doubted his mother would see it that way. Deep in thought, he opened the gate and entered the farmyard, sending Dancer's flock of geese scurrying away with loud cackles.

At once Margery appeared. "Ben, where have you been?" she cried. "Mother was about to go looking for you!" His sister came up and took his arm, and together they walked towards the house.

But it was not their mother who raised the biggest objection to Ben's part in the trap: it was Dancer.

"I never heard such foolishness!" he cried. "What's Stubbs thinking of? I told you – the man's useless!"

They sat around the kitchen table: Margery, Edward and Mary Button, Dancer and Ellen May. All were shocked by Ben's news, but none spluttered like Dancer did. Patiently Ben explained that the trap had been his idea; that he knew how to pass himself off as a stable lad and, besides, the murderer would be surrounded as soon as he got near...

"Stuff and nonsense!" Dancer snorted. "This danger's too serious for Stubbs to deal with. What use are villagers with sickles and pitchforks against a swordsman who has already killed folk?" He blew out his cheeks like a frog. "We should send word to the Sheriff of Middlesex – to London even, to the Queen's Council. They can despatch soldiers on horseback to hunt this villain down like a dog!"

"There isn't time," Ben told him. "Sam thinks Scanes will come tonight. So does the justice."

"That old fool?" Dancer exclaimed. "Why, he

scarce knows whether it's day or night!" He appealed to Mary Button. "Can you make the boy see sense?" he asked. "For I'm sure I can't!"

With hopes faltering, Ben met his mother's eye. He half-expected her to agree with Dancer, but instead she said: "Did Sam give his word that he wouldn't let Scanes near you?"

"He swore he would put my life above his own," Ben answered. "There will be men hidden on every side. All I have to do is wait in the stable, dressed like Hal."

No one spoke. Ben glanced at Edward, but his brother kept his eyes down. Margery and Ellen looked alarmed, as Mary was, despite her calm. But Ben sensed something else in the looks the women exchanged. It reminded him of the last time he had been there. And when Ellen spoke, he breathed a silent sigh of relief.

"Ben knows what to do, Father," she said. "He understands the risk, and what he says makes sense. Scanes must be caught, for everyone's sake. Have you a better plan?"

Dancer frowned. "That's enough cheek from you, mistress," he said. "No one's asking *you* to arm yourself and lie in wait for a murderer, as men like me must do!" But now his protest sounded like mere bluster, and he knew it. In fact it sounded worse than that – and Ben understood why.

"Why are you staring at me?" Dancer demanded, frowning at him. "It's you I'm thinking of – you and everyone else in the village! We haven't faced a threat like this before and, like I've said a hundred times, Stubbs isn't up to it!"

Breathing hard, he looked round at each of them before settling his gaze upon Mary. "Don't you fret," he said. "I'll answer the call, and be at the justice's house. So it's Dancer May who'll be keeping an eye on Ben, to see he comes to no harm. That way we'll not be beholden to Sam Stubbs for anything – will we?"

But Mary merely lowered her eyes.

Ben sighed. He had got his way, but he took no satisfaction from it. Now Dancer would be part of the trap too, and Ben knew why: to try and show his mother what a brave man he was.

Even so, Ben knew that Dancer was scared out of his wits!

A half-hour later Ben left Dancer's. He had taken a hasty supper, though with little appetite. Instead of excitement he felt a sense of foreboding now, and not just for his own safety. Suddenly it looked as if so many things could go wrong. What if Scanes never came? he wondered. Supposing he caught sight of one of the lookouts, and guessed there was a trap? It seemed he was as swift and cunning as he was deadly – apart from Midge Martin's hawks, no one had even seen him. Supposing he decided the risk was too great, gave up his quest for the Black Union and went to seek some other prize? If he did, all their plans would be in vain, and this dangerous man would still be at large.

At the gate Ben looked round to wave goodbye to his mother, Margery and Ellen. Dancer was not to be seen, though he had said he would come to Moon's before sunset. Nor was Edward there. Turning away, Ben tramped along the ridge. But a few minutes later, when he was out of sight of the farm, there came a low whistle. He turned sharply – and understood at once why Edward had not been present. Seeing the look on his brother's face, he stopped in surprise.

"That's right," Edward said, hurrying towards him. "If you're going, then I am too!" And before Ben could answer he added: "If you try and stop me, I'll fight you here and now! You'll have to knock me out, like Hal Faraway did you!"

Ben opened his mouth, but Edward cut him short.

"You've had it your own way from the moment you got here," he said. He was out of breath, for he had run ahead to overtake Ben. "I wasn't allowed to take part in any night-time ventures last time," he went on. "Well now I am, whether you like it or not. I've as much right as anyone – try telling me I haven't!"

"Sam won't allow it," Ben said, knowing how feeble that sounded. "He'll send you home—"

"Then I'll circle round and come back!" Edward retorted.

"Edward!" Ben was exasperated. "Think about Mother – she'll be at her wits' end when she finds you gone. So will Margery—"

"They won't!" Edward cried, with a look of triumph. "They're going home to be with Granny. They think I'm staying at Dancer's with Ellen!"

Ben started to speak...then he saw the knife that was stuck in Edward's belt.

Edward followed his gaze, and nodded. "It was Father's old paring knife. I kept it, when the other tools went."

And there he stood, with fists clenched. He was not going to back down – and all at once Ben had no desire to argue. He was not angry. Instead, to his surprise there was a lump in his throat.

"I'm walking on to the justice's," he said at last. "I won't look behind to see if you're following. In fact, I haven't seen you at all – is that understood?" Without waiting for a reply he started forward. "I don't know how Mother will react," he said over his shoulder. "But I've an idea what Father would have said."

Then quickly he walked away, gaining pace as he went.

Chapter Fifteen

*D*arkness came swiftly. Even the night-time
birds were quiet, as if they too sensed the fear
hanging over Hornsey village. The bark of a fox from
the depths of Tottenham Wood was the only sign that
any creature was abroad that night. People barred
their doors and sat up with such weapons as they
could find. But, in the stable yard at Justice Moon's,
there was an air of quiet determination.

The village men who had come to do their part may
have been afraid, but they did not show it. Roger
Graves was there, though without Gimlet. So was

Isaac Cutter, and others who had taken part in the search two nights before. They gathered about Sam to receive their instructions, and no man argued when he was assigned his place – even Dancer. There was little to be said: by now every one of them knew the danger he might face.

As the watchmen found places to conceal themselves, Ben changed into the old shirt and breeches Sam had borrowed for him, and climbed the ladder to the stable loft. He did not have his dagger, for it might seem odd for a stable boy to carry one. Hal's bed of straw by the wall was as he had left it, covered with an old horse blanket. There was no other sign that he had stayed there. The boy arrived with nothing, Doll Fisher had told Ben, and he took nothing away with him.

Doll was in the house with the doors barred. She refused to go to bed, saying if anyone broke in she would prefer to be in her kitchen. She scorned the justice's idea of loading up his old pistol, which led to another exchange of insults between the two of them. Sam left them to it and went to the stable loft. By the light of a lantern, he crouched beside Ben's pallet.

"I'll be over there in the shadows, where I can see anyone who climbs the ladder," he said. "But he won't see me!"

Ben glanced at the far corner, where an intruder would have to enter through the opening in the floor. He had expected to be on tenterhooks but, now that the trap was laid, he found he was oddly calm.

"Where's Dancer?" he asked.

"Down in the stable with Roger," Sam answered. "They're well prepared." He put his hand on Ben's shoulder. "If Scanes comes...*when* he comes, we'll be ready for him." He frowned. "Though I'm still not happy about using you as bait!"

"It's just another acting role, Sam," Ben said. Putting on his best country accent, he added: "So don't 'e fret, master. Get ye gone now, so I can 'ave a bit of a rest!"

Sam grunted, but managed a quick smile before blowing out the lantern. In the dark, Ben heard him make his way across the floor. There was a rustle of straw as he sat down. And after that, all anyone could do was wait.

But nobody expected they would have to wait all night.

For the first few hours, Ben could not have slept if he tried. He lay stretched out on the pallet, with the straw tickling his feet, listening. He heard Sam move from time to time, but could see almost nothing. It was a clear night, with slivers of starlight showing through holes in the old thatch. Sometimes he heard the scurrying of mice. A bat squeaked as it flittered past the stable and, in the distance, the justice's horse whinnied in the paddock. Ben yawned, remembering Tarlton, the old horse that drew the players' baggage-cart when Lord Bonner's Men went touring. He smiled, picturing Tarlton in his comfortable stable at the White Hart Inn by Bishopsgate. London seemed very far away now. He yawned again. Ben had almost forgotten about Bryn Scanes, and the Black Union, and the fact that he was playing the part of the stable boy. He was very tired. It had been a long wait, but whatever happened he must not fall asleep. Could dawn be approaching already? He sighed, hoping the trap had not been a waste of time. Perhaps Sam was wrong, and their quarry would not come tonight...

Then he gave a shudder, and his eyes opened wide: he had fallen asleep after all.

Ben clenched his fist, digging his nails into his palm. How could he have been so careless! He listened, but all was quiet. He thought of calling out to Sam, then realized how foolish that would be. If the trap was to work everything must appear normal, or Scanes would sense it. Gradually Ben relaxed, and tried to keep his eyes on a gap in the thatch. He heard scurrying again...the mice were busy, he thought.

But after another hour had passed, he could not stay awake any longer. Already a grey light was starting to show through the thatch. A louder rustling, somewhere above his head, could not stop his eyes from closing. As he drifted off he heard a thud, and wondered vaguely what it was. The noises that followed made Ben uneasy. He stirred, half-awake, thinking he had heard cries from below. Footfalls came too, and he realized they were on the ladder, or was it the floor?

Then, in an instant, he was wide awake – too late!

A hand was clamped across his mouth, hot breath was on his face – and a voice, cold as steel, spoke in his ear:

"Make one sound, and you're dead!"

Ben went rigid. He blinked, not daring to move, and let his eyes shift to the left... He would have cried out, but all that came from his mouth was a groan, as he gazed upon a face...a face like a skull!

For seconds it swam before his eyes in the faint light, until a slap on his cheek shook him into full alertness.

"Look at me, boy!"

He looked – and looked away again. Slowly, things began to make sense. His gaze strayed upwards. There was a gaping hole in the thatch, which Bryn Scanes had come through. Ben had even heard him drop to the floor, he realized, so...

Sam! He wanted to speak, but nothing came out. But as if in answer, his captor spoke again.

"Not much of a guard, was he – your friend?" He jerked his head towards Sam's corner. "Well, he's lucky – he'll sleep for a few hours. Though I wouldn't like to wake up with his headache!"

Ben breathed a sigh. So Sam was knocked out...but where were the others? He must try to think. He kept still, and avoided looking at the frightful face, lit garishly by the growing light. One glance had been enough.

But once more, Scanes seemed to read his thoughts.

"Look at me again," he said quietly. And tightening his grip, he forced Ben's head round so that they faced each other. Ben held his breath...then he understood.

It was no skull. It was a narrow face, with hollow eyes and a thin mouth, but where the nose should have been were two dark cavities, with only a fleshy ridge above.

"That's right – my nose was sliced off." Scanes wore the cruellest smile Ben had ever seen. "After a small difficulty I had once, in France...like it, do you?"

Ben did not move.

"Come, boy..." Scanes drew back, though his grip did not lessen. "I never knew a stable lad to be so faint hearted."

Finally, Ben managed to nod.

Scanes regarded him for a moment. "So, I was expected, was I?" he said. "Well, I rather thought that might happen. But I've sprung better traps than this one, boy – do you believe me?"

He waited until Ben nodded again.

"Good! Well now, I'd love to gossip a while longer, but it's getting light, so we must hurry. I've gone to a lot of trouble to get here, and I think you know what I've come for – yes?"

This time, Ben thought it best to answer. "Yes, sir," he whispered.

"Very well! Then all you need do is get it, and our business is done." A pale tongue shot out, as Scanes wet his lips. "Afraid?" he asked. "You should be! But I see no need to take your life, stable boy. Do as I ask – bring it to me – then I'll leave you. *Finis!*"

Ben's mind was working faster now. Of course

Scanes had no intention of breaking into the house again – he expected "Hal" to fetch the pearl to him! But since he had guessed it was a trap, surely he knew there were men hiding all around, as Sam had been...

Then a dreadful picture sprang up. Ben imagined Dancer lying senseless too, and the other men. He had heard cries... He swallowed, but the villain's next words gave him his answer.

"You're thinking of the watchmen, playing hide-and-seek down there?" The man gave a throaty chuckle. "Never fear, boy. They'll be far away, clodhopping through the fields. Why not listen for yourself?" And the man took his hand from Ben's mouth, gripped him by the shoulders and jerked him into a sitting position. Ben listened, but all he heard was a faint cry, from a long way off.

"I arranged a little diversion," Scanes explained. "A few sounds to draw them away. Of course they'll realize soon enough, but by then I'll be gone in another direction." He smiled again. "You know nothing of me, boy. If you did, you'd know it'd take more than a feeble trick like this to catch Bryn Scanes!"

Ben kept still, trying not to give away his thoughts. But something had come back to him in a flash:

Granny saying how the man she heard was well spoken. Scanes was not only clever – he was educated. Had he indeed been a gentleman, once?

For the first time, Ben took a proper look at the man who had put fear into the whole village: one who had murdered and robbed, who had overpowered Sam with ease and sent the other watchmen off on a wild goose chase. He saw the tight padded doublet, with puffs of silk pulled through its slits: once an expensive garment, but now soiled from days spent in hiding. He saw the fine leather belt with its sheath and the dagger. Scanes was on one knee, holding the weapon lightly, almost casually – but there was no doubt he would be swift to use it.

There was only one thing Ben could do. As far as this man knew he was Hal Faraway the stable boy – and he must play his role to the hilt. His very life depended on it.

"Mercy, master," he whispered. "I only done as I was told, see...don't hurt me!"

"No wheedling!" Scanes held up a warning finger. "Do as I bid and you won't be hurt. Understood?"

Ben gulped, and said he did.

"Then get up!"

Scanes stood up quickly, and under his watchful eye Ben did the same. He glanced over to where Sam

194

had been, and made out a shape, lying motionless.

But he was not Ben Button, Sam's friend: he was Hal, he must remember, and he must not show too much concern. Scanes did not know him. As long as he stayed being Hal, who knew where the pearl was hidden, he was safe.

"I'll be close behind you," his captor said. "You're a sharp enough lad, I'll wager, so you won't try anything foolish. Now – down the ladder."

Ben crossed the rough boards, put his feet on the ladder and began to descend. Soon he stepped down onto straw – whereupon a sharp stab of pain in his foot made him stagger. He knew he had picked up a splinter, but there was no time to spend on that. For with a thud, Scanes dropped lightly to the ground beside him. The man was as agile as a cat.

Ben turned...then gasped. Not six feet away Roger lay on his back, eyes wide open. His throat had been cut.

"Let that be a lesson to you," Scanes murmured. "There's one who thought he would play the hero!"

Suddenly Ben thought of Dancer, but Scanes put paid to that fear. "The other one fled," he said. "The speed he scuttled off, he'll be at Highgate by now!"

So, Ben realized, he was on his own but for those in the house. Scanes did not intend to go there himself. At least Doll and the justice were safe, for the moment...

"Now listen well!" Scanes's hand descended on Ben's shoulder. "I'm coming to the doorway with you, but no further – just a precaution. You're going into the house to fetch the thing I came for. Bring it to me here. I'll be watching, so if you thwart me—" The man broke off, and waited until Ben looked his way.

"You won't thwart me, will you?" he said menacingly. "For you must know what happened to that weasel Cutter?"

Scanes moved suddenly and Ben stiffened. He had not thought about the man's sword – the one he had used to murder Daniel Cutter – but here it was, leaning against the wall as if it were a hayfork. Scanes must have left it there after dealing with Roger for, of course, it would have hampered him when he climbed onto the roof to drop through and knock Sam senseless.

Ben shuddered, realizing how lucky Sam had been. He watched Scanes lift the weapon, and realized it was probably Justice Moon's old sword; the one that had been stolen from the house! Not that its age mattered: from the way Scanes handled it, he was clearly an expert swordsman.

"Indeed, sir, I does know what 'appened to Dan

Cutter," he answered. *And I saw too,* he could have added. Instead he said: "But the doors to the house be locked. I'll have to get in through a window, see—"

"Then do it!"

The words came like a whip crack, and Ben saw there was no point in trying to delay. Scanes knew that Hal had hidden the pearl in the house; how Ben got inside was his affair. But as he was about to walk towards the doorway, the villain gripped his shoulder again.

"Wait," he hissed. "First, tell me where you put it!"

Ben gulped – and since there was no time to think of a better answer, he told the truth. "'Tis in the fruit bowl, in my master's study," he said. "It looked a bit like a black cherry, see, so—"

He stopped, as Scanes gave a bark of laughter.

"Among the cherries!" The man shook his head, as if it was the best joke he had heard. "So I walked around it, searching high and low, with one eye on that stupid bird…" His laughter ceased as quickly as it began. "Well, you're a cunning lad," he went on. "'Tis pity I work alone. I could use someone like you!" He sniffed. "No matter – off you go, and retrieve that black cherry! Make sure you find the right one!"

Ben moved to the doorway, trying to ignore the pain in his foot. But as he went, there was a sound from behind that made him eager to be gone. It was a song, sung in a high, soft voice – one Ben knew he would never be able to forget for as long as he lived:

"When as the rye reach to the chin,
And chop-cherry, chop-cherry ripe within,
Strawberries swimming in the cream,
And schoolboys playing in the stream..."

Chapter Sixteen

Trying to look like a burglar, Ben crossed the stable yard stealthily and made his way to the laboratory window. The cobblestones were ice cold beneath his feet. He did not need to turn around – he could feel the man's eyes on him. The house was quiet. He heard the dawn birdsong, but no voices: the watchmen must be far away. He gritted his teeth, realizing how they had underestimated Bryn Scanes. Dancer may be a coward, he thought, but he had been right about one thing: the fellow was more than a match for plain folk like Sam.

Reaching the window, he crouched – then remembered he had no dagger. He hesitated, wondering how close the justice was...should he try to warn him? Or should he tell Scanes he needed a tool to force the catch? Then he took a deep breath: whatever happened, he resolved, he would not go back. He must try to think what to do.

But the next moment he received a jolt, as a low voice hissed at him from just a few feet away.

"Don't look round. Lift your right arm if he's watching you."

It was Edward.

Slowly, Ben raised his arm, as if he were feeling around the window frame.

"Now smash the glass!"

Ben's eyes slid to his left. He saw a large water butt – Edward must be hiding behind it.

Fool! he wanted to shout, but suddenly, his brother's wild idea gave Ben a sliver of hope. At least it would raise the alarm and perhaps, between the two of them...

There was no time to think. Pushing doubts aside, he stood up and slammed his elbow against the window. The crash of breaking glass sounded like the crack of doom.

At first nothing happened. Shards of glass tinkled

on the laboratory floor. Silence followed. The curtain was back, but there was no light within. Ben stared at the broken window, wondering if he could climb through it...

Then footfalls sounded – and he spun round, to see Scanes leaping towards him, sword in hand.

One look at the man was enough: he was furious, his disfigured face terrible in the dawn light. He opened his mouth, and a sound came out that chilled Ben's blood; it was like the cry of an enraged animal.

But unexpectedly another noise came – from inside the house! "Fall to your knees," a voice cried, "or I will shoot!"

It was Justice Moon. And at his shout, Ben took heart. He stepped back as Scanes halted before the window, his face a mask of rage.

"Drop your sword and kneel!" the Justice called loudly. "Or face the consequences!"

But Scanes did not kneel. And, for Ben, what followed was like a dumbshow on the stage – slowed down, as if everyone were moving at half speed. He saw Scanes lower his sword arm, but the man's left hand went to his belt. Out came his dagger, but even as he flung it through the gaping window, there came a roar and a flash of flame. The justice had fired his old pistol. His aim was poor, however, or perhaps his hand had shaken, for the ball whistled over Scanes's head. Unluckily for the justice, Scanes's aim was true: to Ben's dismay there came a cry from inside the study, then the sound of someone falling to the floor. From further off, bizarrely, came the screech of Moon's parrot.

"See what you've done! Go away!"

Scanes whirled round. Again Ben looked into that terrible face – and read his own death...

Until Edward leaped up from behind the water butt, and threw his knife.

There was a hiss of air followed by a soft thud, and Scanes's body jerked. His sword arm drooped and, with a puzzled expression, the murderer turned to look at the old knife that had once belonged to Peter Button, blacksmith, and which was now sticking out of his left shoulder.

"So, there's another—"

The man stood very still, and spoke calmly, as he grew aware of the red stain that was spreading through his doublet. "It was unforeseen...but no matter."

Deliberately he switched his sword from his right hand to his left. With his right he gripped the knife, took a quick breath, and pulled it out.

Both boys froze, half-crouching, but Scanes made no sound of pain. Instead he leaned forward to look through the window. Then, apparently satisfied with what he saw, he faced Ben.

"Climb in and get the pearl, boy," he said through his teeth. "There's nothing to stop you. Did you think I would give up as easily as that?"

Then he smiled his terrible, cruel smile. With a careless movement he tossed the knife into the water butt. Then he levelled his sword at Edward.

"You will kneel," he said icily.

Edward swallowed, but stayed on his feet.

"Down!" Scanes snapped.

Still Edward did not move. Ben's fear was unbearable – not for himself, but for his brother. Desperately, he tried to think – whereupon another voice, one he had all but forgotten about, came through the window.

"Murderer! You touch either of them, and I'll chop your ear off!"

Scanes swung round, as did Ben, and his heart leaped. Doll Fisher was standing at the window with a huge butcher's knife in her fist. She was trembling, but her gaze was steady.

"You heard me!" Doll shouted. "This edge is razor-sharp..." She glanced at Ben and Edward. "You boys back away!" she cried. "I've signalled to the guard – the place will be swarming with men in no time!"

Nobody moved. Ben knew Doll was bluffing, for there were no watchmen within earshot, but Scanes could not be certain of that. The four of them stood in silence, as if playing the old game to see who would blink first, until Ben heard a very welcome sound indeed: footsteps from the stable.

Sam appeared in the doorway. He had only his wooden billet, and looked unsteady on his feet, but it was enough. Suddenly the odds had tilted against Scanes, and he knew it. He stiffened, his head swinging from Sam, to Doll at the window, and back to Ben and Edward...

Then he struck.

The sword rose in an arc, glittering as the sun's first ray caught it. The blade came down...only to strike the cobblestones with a shriek and produce a shower of sparks. Then it clattered to the ground. It had missed Edward by a whisker, because Scanes had staggered.

The brothers watched the villain step back, hissing with pain, which must have hit him in a rush from the effort of lifting his arm. Blood ran from his wound, dripping to the stones...

But the drama wasn't over yet.

Scanes was hurt, and he had lost his sword; Sam could overpower him now – as could the two boys, or a woman with a kitchen knife. But Scanes could not yield now, for it meant his certain death. All he could do was gather what strength he had, and run.

He started towards the path by the house – his best route of escape – but Sam moved to block his way. "It's no use," the miller breathed. "There are lookouts between here and the wood. You'll never reach it!"

For a second Scanes wavered. Then he lashed out at Sam, sending him staggering backwards. As Sam fell, the murderer turned and ran in the other direction. He veered past Ben and Edward, rounded the stable wall and was lost to sight. Ben knew there was a low fence behind, then fields beyond. After that the ground rose, westwards towards the Hog's Back.

"I'll get after him!" It was the first time Edward had spoken since telling Ben to smash the window. "Send help quickly!"

"Don't be foolish!" Ben cried. He felt relief that Scanes had gone, but alarm that his brother meant to follow him.

"You're barefoot, Master Ben," Doll called through the window. "Let Edward go – he can move faster, and track the rogue!"

"That's right," Edward said, already moving away. He was strong and fast on his feet. Ben stared after him. Even though his brother had come close to death, the light Ben had seen in his eyes was from excitement rather than fear. "You see to Sam and the justice, and get help as fast as you can," Edward called back. "Scanes can't run far, the state he's in!"

But Ben could not let Edward go alone. He started to follow – then limped suddenly, as pain shot through his foot once again. The splinter – he must get rid of it first... Wincing, he could only watch as his brother sped away.

Moving to deal with the situation, Ben helped Sam to sit up. There was a lump on the miller's head the size of an egg, but he was soon on his feet. "I'll raise a hue and cry," he said, and was quickly gone from the yard.

It was the justice who gave most concern – so there was relief when it turned out he was not badly wounded. Scanes's dagger had been aimed at his heart, but when Moon had raised his hand to fire his pistol, the knife had missed its target and gashed his forearm instead. The man was weak from the shock, but would recover. They sat him in the kitchen, and Doll fussed about, scolding him.

Ben was restless, and worried about Edward. In a way, he felt responsible for what had happened. If he had not fallen asleep when he did... Biting his lip, he hunted around for something pointed to get the splinter out of his foot. Finding a small skewer, he sat on the floor and busied himself with the task, while Doll bandaged the justice's arm.

"You're lucky to be alive," she was muttering. "That old pistol of yours couldn't hit a wall – you should thank your stars it didn't explode in your face!"

"My stars?" the justice mumbled. "It's Master Buttermilk I should thank, and his brother...and you too, I suppose."

Doll snorted. "What about Sam Stubbs? He's another one lucky to be alive." Her face darkened. "Unlike poor Roger Graves..." She sniffed, and glanced at Ben. "Now, you stop blaming yourself," she said. "That murderous wretch outwitted the lot of them – you could have been killed, too! The trap was a fool's game from the start—"

She broke off as the back door opened. Sam came in, out of breath.

"I've got men together," he said to the justice. "They're looking all over – he can't have got far." Sam gestured to the open door. "And we've got more help, if you want it."

When Moon looked puzzled, Sam went to the doorway and beckoned. Midge Martin appeared outside, with a hooded hawk on his wrist.

"He won't come in," Sam said. "You know what he's like. But he says he can send his goshawk up, to spy out the land."

Midge stood calmly in the yard. Seeing the justice get slowly to his feet, he inclined his head and waited.

"Master Martin?" Moon stood at the door. "We would indeed value your help. A hawk's eye is better than a man's."

"I can't make promises, sir," Midge said. "But I can let Juno circle the village. I believe I'll know if it's only prey she sees – or if it's something else."

"I thank you most heartily," Moon replied. He watched as the old hawksman nodded and walked off. But when he turned to Doll, he was taken aback by her expression.

"What are you staring at, woman?" he demanded.

Doll threw Ben a glance before replying. "I was wondering if you knocked your head on something, when you fell."

The justice grunted. "I fear Martin's goshawk will be of little use," he said, ignoring Doll's remark. "No doubt he understands the bird's ways, but it cannot tell him what it sees. Precious time may be lost if people start watching the hawk."

Suddenly, Ben sensed that something important was coming. He had managed to draw the fearsome splinter from his foot at last, and stood up. To his relief, the pain was only slight. He had his shoes ready, but as he pulled them on, he saw the justice nod to himself, and seem to come to a decision.

"I will trust you, Master Button, as the parson trusted you," Moon went on. "But if I swear you to secrecy I expect you to keep your word. Do you understand?"

"I always keep my word, sir," Ben answered.

"Very well." Moving towards the passage door, the justice gestured for Ben to follow him. As they stepped outside, Ben looked back to see Doll gazing at them – but at the justice's next words, his own jaw dropped.

"There's something I want to show you that might tell us which way the fugitive has fled," he said quietly. "You may help me operate it, but you must speak of it to no one. Indeed, you must forget all about it, for word of its very existence may put me and my household in mortal danger."

And with a gleam in his eye, he added: "It's in the upstairs room that I always keep locked."

Chapter Seventeen

The room was at the south-east corner of the house, with a window in the front and side walls. Despite all that had happened, and the urgency of his need to help Edward, Ben was intrigued as he watched Master Moon take a key from the pocket of his gown and unlock the door. The final mystery, it seemed, would become clear at last – but when he followed the justice inside, he was surprised to find the room almost empty. There was a table with charts and drawing instruments on it, but nothing more. Then the justice closed the door and moved aside –

to reveal the strangest object Ben had ever seen.

His first thought was that it was a firearm, though the barrel was rather long...and, in any case, there was no stock or trigger. It was fixed on a wooden stand at a slight angle, pointing to the window. But when Ben peered in the top of the barrel, his eyes widened: there was glass in it! Nor was it a barrel, but a narrow cylinder made of what looked like ox-horn. He looked round, to see the justice watching him.

"You may count yourself privileged, Master Button," he said. "For apart from myself, and the clever man who made it, you are the first person to see my *perspective glass!*"

Ben looked again, then understood. "I saw sunlight, reflected off the end of it!" he exclaimed. "It was the day I arrived. I thought someone was at the window, watching me."

"Likely I was adjusting it," Moon replied. "Or cleaning the lens. I mainly use it at night." Indicating that Ben should move to the lower end of the tube, he pointed at it.

"I know of no other instrument like this in all England – yet. But in Europe men of science are working on them, better to observe the skies. The lenses are of Venetian glass, fashioned by spectacle-makers – but the craftsman who built this was

Dutch." He put his hand on the cylinder, as if caressing it. "There was also an Englishman – Master Digges, who is said to have produced a device more than twenty years ago. To my regret, I never saw it."

The justice seemed to have forgotten everything but his perspective glass, and Ben had to reign in his impatience. How was this going to help Edward? he wondered – until the justice spoke again. And soon, things began to make sense. "There are two lenses in the barrel," Moon went on. "That's why the image is upside down when you look through it – something one must get used to. I'd like three lenses, to bring it the right way up – and to increase magnification. Perhaps one day..." He stood back. "But here, look for yourself!"

So Ben put his eye to the lens – and gasped.

"Trees!" he cried. "But they're—"

"Upside down, as I said," Moon broke in. "Try to imagine the picture the other way up."

Ben looked again. He was observing Tottenham Wood. The treetops were at the bottom of his field of vision, and the trunks at the top. Then he realized that they looked bigger, because the glass made them appear closer.

"It magnifies four times only," the justice was saying. "But that is a joy to a man who yearns to observe the stars and planets, and map the heavens. Now, do you begin to see what a wondrous device a perspective glass is?"

Ben took his eye from the lens. "I do, sir," he replied. "And I see why folk believe you read the stars by magic."

"Let them think what they like!" Moon retorted. "Perhaps you can understand why I keep the device secret. Already I'm rumoured to be a conjuror who meddles in the black arts!" He was indignant, but managed to collect himself. "Well, perhaps one day people will know better," he went on. "Until then I will work alone, and keep my own counsel. But I do not practise magic – only scientific observation!"

"I understand, sir," Ben said. "So may we now train the glass, and see what we can find?"

To his relief, the justice nodded and grew businesslike. "The lenses have a few bubbles in them," he went on. "But your eyes will grow accustomed. I'm certain they're better than mine. Why else do you think I brought you here?"

Eagerly, Ben put his eye to the lens again. Then, with Moon guiding him at first, he began to rotate the instrument.

Slowly he turned it away from the trees, until it pointed south-east along the road, then southwards across open fields. It squealed on its swivel mounting, but remained steady when Ben stopped it. To his disappointment, however, he saw only a brown-and-green blur.

"It's like a mist," he said.

"You must draw the sleeve out," Moon told him. "Here, let me do it."

Ben watched him slide out another barrel that fitted snugly inside the outer casing. He adjusted it, peered through it, then stood back. When Ben looked again, the image was clear.

"I see the fields!" he exclaimed. "And the cows. But nothing else...no people, I mean."

"Make a sweep, from east to west," the justice said. "Up and down too."

Ben did so. Gradually he became used to the upside-down picture, remembering to move upwards to view the fields, rather than downwards, which showed him only blue sky. Once the sun dazzled him, but quickly he moved the glass further to his right, towards the Hog's Back, until suddenly everything went black. He had turned it too far and now faced the wall, which was panelled with dark oak.

"There's nothing for it," the justice muttered. "We'll have to open the window. Someone may see us, but that's a risk I must take."

He threw open the casement. Helped by Ben, he moved the stand forward as far as it would go, tilted the glass and poked it through the opening. Then, at Moon's bidding, Ben put his eye to the lens again.

Now he could see further – quite a lot further. He saw Dancer's fields, and the yard; were those white dots geese? Soon he would see the farmhouse. He wondered why he hadn't spotted any search parties. Perhaps they were on the other side of the village. His eye was watering now and he was about to look away, when something moved.

It was a dark speck…was it a horse? Or was it one of the bubbles Moon had spoken of? Then Ben cried out. "Scanes! I see him, he's behind Dancer's farm! He must have given them the slip!"

Excitedly he turned to Moon, but the justice was frowning. "He's making for the path to Crux End. If he skirts the village and reaches the Toll Road, he'll get clear away!"

"No he won't," Ben said at once. "Because I'm going after him!"

And with that he bounded past the justice, pulled open the door and darted outside. As he ran, a voice called after him:

"Remember your oath! Say the hawk spied him – not my glass!"

In minutes Ben was racing across the stubble fields, ignoring his sore foot. What he would do when he caught up with Scanes, he did not yet know. But of one thing he was certain: he was not going to stop until he did.

He reached the Hog's Back, and Dancer's farm. When he was almost at the gate he slowed down. He was sure he had seen the fugitive above the farm, moving south-west. But suppose he was hiding somewhere, waiting to pounce?

"Ben – wait!"

Looking to his left, Ben saw a figure vault over the gate and hurry towards him. It was Edward.

"I'm onto him," Ben gasped, catching his breath. "He was spotted, behind the farm. He's making for Crux End!"

"I knew he came this way!" Edward cried. "I saw drops of blood in the stubble, but when I got up here I lost him. He must have run like a wounded stag!"

"If Scanes has gone to ground," Ben said, "it won't be a stag we face – more like a cornered wolf."

"Well, at least I've got this!" Edward was holding an old reaping hook, that looked as if it would barely cut corn...but, all at once, Ben's heart lifted. It was the first time he had seen his brother smile since he had returned home.

There was no time to waste, however. Without further word both boys started off along the fence, and rounded the corner of Dancer's barn. Then, side by side, they settled into a steady trot, following the Hog's Back.

To their right the land sloped down to the village; to their left it gave way to open meadow. Soon Sam's mill was ahead, with his hut beside it. Sensing danger, both boys slowed down

"He can't have got to Crux End yet," Edward said. "He was losing blood—" Then he broke off, as Ben peered downwards.

"He still is."

Edward too saw the crimson droplets, glistening on the ground. "Fresh," he muttered, glancing up at Sam's tumbledown cottage. "I can't see where else he could hide, up here."

"Nor me," Ben agreed.

They eyed the cottage cautiously. For all Ben knew, Scanes had already seen them. He had lost his sword and dagger, but Ben's short acquaintance with the man was enough to make him very wary. The odds may have been in the brothers' favour, yet...

"I can get round the back," Edward said suddenly. "I could climb on the roof like he did, at the justice's. Lucky I saw him, wasn't it? If I'd gone chasing after the others, who knows what might have happened. Anyway if I do that, you—"

"You don't think we'll be as lucky as that again, do you?" Ben broke in. "He could be watching us right now!"

"So what's your plan?" Edward countered. "One of us keeps an eye on the place, while the other runs to find Sam? Suppose Scanes breaks cover?"

Ben hesitated, scanning the fields...then pointed. To the north-west, above the Bramble Bush Inn, a large bird was hovering. As Edward followed Ben's finger, the hawk made a swoop, circled and hovered again – closer than before. Then, to the relief of both boys, from beyond the inn came distant shouts.

"You can run faster than me," Ben said. "I'll keep watch—"

But he fell silent, hearing the bang of a door. Both of them looked round sharply – to see a figure jump down the mill's steps.

"Too late!" Edward cried. "Come on!"

Off he sped like a hare, and all Ben could do was stumble after him. Scanes had not been hiding in

Sam's cottage: he must have been inside the mill, gathering his strength, and now he had indeed broken cover!

Edward flew across the grass, reducing the distance from perhaps thirty yards to twenty, then ten. Scanes was loping ahead, without looking back. It was uncanny how he could still run so fast, Ben thought, but now, he saw the man was weakening. His pace was slower...he stumbled once, but stayed on his feet. In seconds they would catch him, but what then? Was the search party within earshot? Perhaps if Ben shouted loudly enough...

The distance was but a few yards now; in a moment Edward would be upon the man. Then suddenly Scanes fell to his knees, and Edward checked his stride. But as Ben drew alongside his brother, their quarry turned sharply – and both of them stopped dead.

Once again Ben looked upon that dreadful face, now running with sweat and streaked with dust from the mill. Scanes looked like a ghostly creature from some terrible netherworld. Again Ben saw the man's fine doublet with the puffs of gold silk, now drenched with blood...then he froze.

They had assumed Scanes was unarmed – but they were wrong. Too late, they saw the small pocket-dagger in his hand. Edward gulped, swung his foolish reaping hook...and missed by inches.

Scanes ducked, forcing himself to his feet. The man was hissing with pain and fatigue, and had no breath to waste on speech – then suddenly he stiffened, and Edward cried out.

The dagger flashed in the sunlight – but it met only empty air. By a miracle Edward managed to dodge aside, and the man's aim was wild. But Edward's luck was short-lived, for in recovering his balance he lost his grip on the hook. And even as it fell, Scanes gathered strength for another thrust...

Then, snapping to his senses, Ben kicked out, and caught Scanes on the knee.

There was a crack as his blow connected with the man's kneecap. Scanes's breath flew from his mouth. Savagely he made another sweep with the dagger... but his legs gave way. With a cry, this most terrible of foes sagged and fell face down. Without waiting, Ben darted forward and pinned the man's dagger-hand to the ground – then to his relief, he realized Scanes had no strength left. He turned to Edward, who was staring open-mouthed.

"Will you get the blade off him?" Ben asked, rather shakily.

Edward's chest was heaving, but he stepped

forward. He stooped – then gave a start and drew back.

"He's...at least, I think..." He swallowed.

Ben drew a sharp breath. He knew Scanes had lost a great deal of blood from his injuries...so he too stepped back, letting the man's limp hand free.

Both of them stood aghast, dimly aware of shouts growing closer as the search party ran uphill towards them. But even when the men reached the brothers, and someone shouted to them to stand clear, neither boy could take his eyes off the blood-soaked figure lying in the stubble at their feet. Finally Ben looked up, and saw Sam.

"Look out – he's alive!" Sam shouted.

In that second, writhing like a snake, Scanes had rolled away from the boys. He struggled to his feet and, when he raised his face – as baleful as a wildcat's – the onlookers fell back in alarm. Desperately he struck out with his dagger, but it was no use: his strength was gone. He made one last, hopeless lunge before his knees buckled. The men began to breathe more easily – until Scanes's last act caught everyone unawares.

All at once the villain reversed his dagger, so that its point was directly above his heart. There were gasps of horror as he fell forward upon it. A hoarse, rattling breath escaped from his mouth, then he lay still.

In the shocked silence, a white-haired man stepped forward to peer down at the body. It was Isaac Cutter, still panting from his uphill climb.

"'Tis fitting that such a creature as this should deal his own death blow," Isaac murmured. "Now he has paid for what he did to my son."

He sighed, and looked at Ben. "You boys did brave work," he added. "And you've earned my gratitude, for as long as I live."

But Ben let his eyes drift upwards, to where Midge Martin's goshawk was hovering above their heads.

"The hawk did the work," he said. "Her eyes are sharper than ours. We followed, and were lucky."

He glanced at Edward, who wore a look of surprise. But, seeing Ben's expression, he kept silent.

Chapter Eighteen

The danger had passed, like a storm that had lasted for days. Hornsey could return to being the sleepy village Ben knew, and would miss. He was thinking about it some days after the events on the Hog's Back, when things had quietened down. Having bade farewell to the neighbours, he was going home to pack his belongings. John Symes had sent word by messenger that he would arrive the next day to collect him.

Ben closed the door of Widow Luce's cottage after saying his goodbye. He was sorry that the widow's little casket had never been found, but since Ben's part in catching Bryn Scanes was now the talk of the village, she had been glad to see him. There was respect in her eyes as she wished him well in London.

The funerals of Roger Graves and Daniel Cutter had taken place two days previously. The village was in mourning, yet people were keen to get back to their old lives. But some things, Ben knew, would never be the same.

The day before, he had been called to Justice Moon's house. The laboratory was back in order and the window mended, but this time Ben did not go in there. The justice had taken him to the garden, where his new gardener was at work. The old tree trunk that had blocked the gateway was gone, cut up for firewood. A new stable lad had been engaged, as well as a maid to help Doll in the house.

"Mistress Fisher gave me a choice," the justice had grumbled. "Either I make some improvements, or I lose the best servant I've ever had. Even if she is the rudest!"

Ben was pleased that Justice Moon realized how brave Doll Fisher had been. He would never forget how she had stood by the window with a butcher's knife, facing up to Scanes. There was another addition to the justice's household too: Doll had insisted that he give Roger's dog, Gimlet, a new home. It was the least they could do, she'd said.

Bryn Scanes had not been buried in the graveyard of St Mary's church, alongside Daniel Cutter and Roger Graves. His body was placed in a coffin and kept in the crypt while Parson Harrington made enquiries, for no one knew where the man came from. It would not be until long after Ben was back in London that he would learn the truth: how Scanes was the wayward son of a knight, who had gone astray. He had ended up at sea on an English warship, where he had gained a reputation as a thief and a cheat. He had come to be so horribly injured after a fight in the French port of Marseilles.

By chance, a few years after Sir Francis Drake's prize the *San Felipe* was brought into Plymouth, Scanes found himself in Newgate Prison with a man who had got hold of a precious jewel from the treasure hoard: a petty thief from Hornsey, named Daniel Cutter. And that, Ben would learn, was how the man's desire to get his hands on the Black Union had started the train of events that led to Cutter's murder, and to Scanes's death on the Hog's Back. When his story became known, Parson Harrington arranged for Scanes's body to be delivered to his family, which was a relief to the whole village.

There were other things that pleased Ben. In reward for Sam's service, Justice Moon had allowed him to resign as constable and go back to running his mill. So once again the village was without an officer of the law. Some said that this was perhaps as well, since none of the villagers wanted to form watch parties again; and Dancer May was the most reluctant of all! Dancer had kept out of sight since the day Scanes had been killed. Only Ellen was seen about the village.

"So, Master Buttermilk – I mean, Master Button..." Moon had fixed Ben with his stern gaze. "The village owes you its thanks for your courage – but, most of all perhaps, for your quick thinking. I suppose there's no point in my inviting you to stay and help me with my observations? Remember: the pursuit of knowledge is the finest calling a man can have!"

Ben had thanked him, explaining that he had another calling: he was a player at heart, and his master would be coming to fetch him soon. So all Justice Moon had been able to do was to shake Ben's hand, and remind him of his oath: to keep the perspective glass a secret. As Ben had walked from the old house, the last thing he heard was the parrot through an open window: *"See what you've done? Go away!"*

Now, as he walked back to the old forge, Ben could

smile about it, yet his heart was heavy at the thought of taking leave of his mother, Margery and Edward. They had had so little time to talk...but then, who could have imagined what would happen almost as soon as Ben had arrived? He was beginning to wonder whether danger followed him around, like an old enemy, waiting to challenge him at every turn. What next? he wondered.

The street was quiet as he walked to his house. Already the summer was waning. The second harvest would take place soon but, as Edward had predicted, Ben would not be there to help. He was opening the door when Margery appeared. Taking his arm, she drew him indoors. "There are surprises for you," she said. "And this time I won't let the cat out of the bag!"

It was midday, and there was food on the table. There were also two small parcels wrapped in cloth at the place where Ben usually sat. His mother drew near, smiling at him. "One's from Granny," she said. "The other is...well, look for yourself."

Ben unwrapped Granny Jenkin's package, and found a stoneware jar. Tied to it was a scrap of paper, on which the old woman had written in her crabbed hand:

DAMSONS FOR MY CLEVER GRANDSON. CAN BE MADE INTO TARTS.

There was a lump in Ben's throat. He had already been to Tottenham Wood, to say farewell to Granny. Willing hands were putting the cottage in order. By good fortune, some of her jars of preserves were undamaged – and here was one of them.

"Open the other one," Mary said. Ben put down the damsons. The other parcel was not wrapped in linen like Granny's jar, but in black cloth. He unfolded it and took out a small book, neatly bound, with gold letters on the front.

The Old Wives' Tale, he read. *By Master George Peele.*

But when he opened it, and saw what was written inside in a fine scholar's hand, he let out a gasp.

To my brightest pupil, Master B. Button, who acted in this play with the Lord Bonner's Men. From his friend and tutor, Robert Harrington.

Ben looked up. "He came by a while ago," his mother told him. "He said he saw it in a bookseller's in London. He must have bought it for you last week…"

"When he went to find out about the Black Union!" Margery finished. She was still amazed by the tale of the giant pearl that had travelled round the world to end up in her village. The Black Union had been sent to Harrington's friend, the jeweller, who would see it restored to the Queen. As for a reward…well, the folk of Hornsey would have to wait.

But Ben barely heard his sister. Although he could read well enough, he had never owned a book before. All he ever saw of the plays he performed in was his own part, and the prompt sheets Will Sanders pinned up in the tiring room. He stared at his copy of *The Old Wives' Tale* – until the door swung open, and Edward came in.

"I hope you've had a nice morning," he said to Ben. "Some of us had work to do!"

But Ben saw the glint in his brother's eye. "I didn't want to get in your way," he said. "We town boys are no use on a farm, are we?"

They had not spoken about the farm lately. They had not spoken about Dancer either, but it was clear things had changed. Dancer's flight from Justice Moon's stable, leaving Roger to die at Scanes's hands, was known throughout the village. Folk shook their heads: let the man's own shame be his punishment, they said.

Edward had still gone to work at the farm these past days, but he came home to eat dinner. Now, he exchanged a glance with his mother.

"The surprises aren't quite over yet," she told Ben. "Edward's got some news for you." Ben turned expectantly, to see his brother looking embarrassed.

"I've been thinking," Edward said. "About a lot of things. Father, for one...and things you said and, well, with all that's happened—" He trailed off. Whereupon Margery could stand it no longer, and blurted out: "He's not going to work for Dancer any more! He's going as prentice to the blacksmith in Crux End! Then when he's finished his prenticeship he's going to come back and open up the forge! Hornsey will have a smith again – Edward Button!"

Now Ben was truly lost for words. He gazed at his brother.

"Like I said, with all that's happened—" Edward was going red now. But Ben laughed aloud from sheer relief.

"That's the best surprise of all," he said.

The others smiled, even Edward, but Ben's smile faded as another thought sprang up. He turned to his mother to see her flushing as Edward had done. It was a Button family trait.

"That's enough gossip," she said quickly. "You boys go out and wash – Margery, haven't you forgotten something?"

"The cheese!" Margery exclaimed, and hurried to fetch it.

Ben and Edward went outside. In the garden, as they washed from the same pail, Ben spoke up. "I don't know what to say," he murmured. "Except that I'm...well, I'm proud of you—" But he broke off, as Edward seized the bucket and stood back.

"One more word, and it won't be your city shoes that get wet," he warned. "I'll soak you from head to foot!"

But all Ben did was smile again.

That evening he had time to talk with his mother at last, after Edward and Margery had gone to bed. The night had turned chilly, and Ben lit a small fire in the hearth. The two of them sat, recalling memories of Ben's father – times that now seemed long ago. Ben told his mother a little about his life as a player, while she spoke of Granny and of her sisters. But still it seemed as if one subject must not be mentioned, until at last, to Ben's relief, his mother raised it herself.

"I don't want you to go away unhappy," she said. "So I'll tell you now. Edward knows, but not Margery – not yet." She drew a breath and said: "I'm not going to marry Dancer. I won't speak about it now," she added. "But I know you'll understand when I say he isn't the man I thought he was."

She looked away, and Ben saw the strain on her face. He knew how hard her decision had been. He badly wanted to speak to her about Sam, but he knew this was not the time. Instead he said: "How will you manage? I mean, I know there's the cow, but—"

"Don't fret about that," Mother said. "There'll be one less mouth to feed when Edward goes to Tom Wilkes the blacksmith. He'll have bed and board there, and his clothes, as you do. Margery and I can get by, and Ellen will still sell our butter and eggs at market. She's a good girl."

She sighed. "Her father's not a bad man. He's never been happy since her mother died, Ellen says. He needs a wife – and he'll find one, sooner or later."

Then she caught the look on Ben's face. "Is there something else troubling you?"

"It's…well, it's those things Dancer said, the first night I was home," he answered. "About players being rogues and liars, and the theatre being no place for a true Englishman…" He swallowed. "Is that what you think, too?"

Mary gazed at Ben – then she shook her head.

"No, it isn't," she said. "And I'm ashamed I let him say those things. But I promise you this: if anyone ever says anything like that again about my brave son, who performs in front of thousands of people – even before the Queen and all her court – I'll knock them down myself!"

At last she smiled, so that in a rush of hope Ben blurted it out. "There's – well, there's another thing too," he began. "It's about Sam..." Then he stopped. "Sorry," he mumbled. "I don't suppose I'm very tactful, am I?"

But the smile remained on his mother's face.

"Go to bed, Ben," she said.

In the morning Ben stood outside the cottage with his pack. He had said goodbye to Edward, who was going to Dancer's for the last time. He would still help with the harvest, he'd told Ben, before he left to be apprenticed to his new master. Edward got the chance to have one last dig about Ben going off to his easy life, but the two had parted with a firm handshake. Ben had watched his brother go off whistling, and turned away to cast his gaze about the street.

Time passed, and a half-hour later he was still there. Surely John, his master, should be here soon? He tried to whistle to himself, but for some reason he couldn't. He wet his lips and tried again – then he heard footsteps.

"So, Master Mutton, do you mean to go off without saying goodbye? That's a fine thing, isn't it!"

Sam had come round the corner of the next cottage,

the one where the village carpenter lived. "I've had business with one of your neighbours," he said. "I thought I'd have a bit of work done on my hut...stop the wind howling through it."

Finding himself short of words, Ben nodded. He tried to whistle again, but still no sound came out. He would miss Sam – then all at once, he was eager to tell him Mary's news.

"There's something you should know," he began. "Mother told me last night. I suppose I shouldn't say anything, but..."

"What's that?" Sam asked, with a puzzled look.

Ben swallowed. "Well, it's a ticklish matter. I was thinking of what you told me, when we were walking back from the justice's that day. And – well, Mother says..."

"Oh, that," Sam sniffed. "I wouldn't worry your head over that business, if I were you."

Ben blinked, then realized the puzzled look had been a sham. His friend laughed, and slapped him on the shoulder.

"And I thought *you* were the player!" he cried. "No matter. I know all about Dancer, and I've been given a hint that I may call upon your mother soon. Does that please you?"

It does, Ben thought. But he shrugged, and said

he supposed it could do no harm. Though how Sam would find the time, when he was always grumbling about how busy he was, he didn't know. And there they stood exchanging jibes, until there was a rattle of wheels, and both turned to look up the street.

A cart appeared, drawn by an old, brown horse. Ben broke into a smile at the sight of the man in the driver's seat. He wore a garish blue doublet and a hat with a jay's feather in it. Ben waved, and John Symes waved back.

A short while later, they drove out of the village.

The farewells were over. Ben had hugged his mother and Margery, and promised to write a letter before Christmas. There were tears from Margery, which she said were because he had forgotten to say goodbye to Eliza. So to please her Ben had hurried down to the pasture, feeling somewhat foolish, and spoken to the cow. Sweaty from running, he had come back to find John standing with Margery, his mother and Sam, along with several villagers who had gathered to watch the event. And at the sight of the people he loved best chatting amiably, Ben had found the lump back in his throat.

To hide it he had tried to whistle again, but still he couldn't. So he had climbed up on the cart, said his last goodbyes, and turned away. He was sad, of course, but he was excited too – as he had been the day he had arrived home, when Master Bowles had thrown his pack down from the cart. Now he was going back to the theatre, and to his other family: Lord Bonner's Men.

Both he and John were quiet as they passed the church, and Tarlton ambled onto the Newington road. As they rolled slowly uphill, John pointed to the big house on their right.

"Whose is that place?" he asked.

Ben told him it belonged to Master Moon, the justice. They drove past, and Ben looked back once at the upstairs window on the corner, glinting in the sunlight. Then he turned sharply, as John drew the cart to a halt.

"Looks as if someone else wants to see you off," he said.

An old man was standing by the roadside. As they stopped, he walked forward and touched his hat in greeting. There was a hooded bird on his gauntlet.

"So, you're leaving us again?" Midge Martin said.

"I am, Master Midge," Ben answered. "But I'm glad to see you. I haven't had chance to say goodbye

– or to thank you for your help."

Midge regarded him for a moment. "A bad business," he said quietly. "But it's over. My hawks can fly in the woods, and all's well." He paused. "Strange how it ended. You and your brother being in the right place, when everyone else was on the other side of the village, eyes peeled for my Juno."

John Symes glanced curiously at the old man. Ben was wondering what to say – until Midge came to his rescue.

"Yet, 'tis no matter," he went on. "Things have a way of settling themselves. You have keen eyes, boy, and you were a step ahead. 'Twas Juno had to catch up with you!"

He gave Ben a shrewd look. "Don't fret," he muttered. "If there was something else…something that helped you spy out the land that day, I shan't speak of it. Let's call it our secret, shall we?" And with that he touched his hat again, and walked off.

John shook the reins and urged Tarlton up the hill. If he had noticed the bruise on Ben's forehead, which was now turning yellow, he did not mention it. Instead he said: "So, has much happened while you've been in Hornsey?"

Ben was looking at the fields, hazy in the sunshine. "Well, it can get a bit turbulent here," he said. "I'm looking forward to being back in London. It's quieter, sometimes."

John gave him a shrewd look. Whatever had happened, he knew Ben would tell him about it when he was ready. Just now, his prentice looked as if he wanted a little peace and quiet.

Some time later, Ben saw a hawk swooping gracefully through the sky. Briefly it hovered overhead, then wheeled and flew away towards Highgate Hill.

He watched it disappear, then he tried to whistle again – and found that he could. He had been whistling for almost a minute, before he realized what the tune was.

"That's 'Chop-cherry Ripe'," John said. "You sang it in *The Old Wives' Tale*, remember?"

"So I did," Ben replied. "I'd almost forgotten."

Then, without expression, he gazed at the road ahead.

About the author

John Pilkington worked in a research laboratory, on a farm, and as a rock guitarist in several bands before realizing he wanted to write. After taking a degree in Drama and English, and acting and directing for a touring theatre company, he began his professional writing career with radio plays. He has since written plays for the theatre and television scripts for the BBC. He is also the author of a series of historical crime novels, and a non-fiction book, *A Survival Guide for Writers*. *Elizabethan Mysteries* is his first series for younger readers.

Born in Lancashire, John now lives in Devon with his partner and son.

For more heart-pounding historical adventures, log on to www.fiction.usborne.com

Usborne Quicklinks

For links to websites where you can find out more about life in Elizabethan England, explore an Elizabethan theatre and learn about Sir Francis Drake and the treasure he captured at sea, go to the Usborne Quicklinks Website at www.usborne-quicklinks.com and enter the keyword "thief".

Internet safety

When using the Internet, make sure you follow these safety guidelines:

- Ask an adult's permission before using the Internet.
- Never give out personal information, such as your name, address or telephone number.
- If a website asks you to type in your name or e-mail address, check with an adult first.
- If you receive an e-mail from someone you don't know, don't reply to it.

Usborne Publishing is not responsible and does not accept liability for the availability or content of any website other than its own, or for any exposure to harmful, offensive, or inaccurate material which may appear on the Web. Usborne Publishing will have no liability for any damage or loss caused by viruses that may be downloaded as a result of browsing the sites it recommends. We recommend that children are supervised while on the Internet.